Fuck a Friend Zone

By

Jaythawriter

D1368813

CHAPTER ONE

" Fuck you, Rome! That's why I'm going to find me a scamming ass nigga! Broke bitch! That hoe can never be me!" A woman by the name Kat yelled. Rome stood and watched as she held a brick in her hands. It was a summer night, and the block was packed with dopeboys, and hood chicks looking for a come up. Rome was the highlight of the evening as the liquor, and good weed had everyone enjoying the show. He stood on the other side of his Mercedes, and Kat stood on the other side with a brick in her hands. She had already keyed the side of his door, and he didn't know why. It was nothing like summertime in Chicago, and tonight proved why that statement was true. It looked like a car show, and the streets were packed. Rome was every woman's catch, standing six-foot-four inches with a peanut butter complexion. They all wanted a piece of him, but Rome wasn't a one-woman kind of man, and now he was paying the price for his hoe ways, and his best friend, Heaven was front row laughing her ass off.

She had an " I told you so," look on her face, Heaven tried to warn him about how crazy Kat was, but he wouldn't listen. Rome was a sucker for a fat ass, and a smile. It was his weakness, and Heaven knew it would end this way. Rome and Heaven had been best friends since the second grade when she stopped a bully from taking Rome's lunch. Many folks have mistaken their friendship for something else, but it was far from anything intimate. They were airtight, and not once had either of them thought about crossing that line. Heaven was in a relationship now, and it was hard for her, because her man wasn't secure with how they were close with each other. It's was merely platonic, and the world wasn't buying it. But it was the truth, and nobody would believe it. It was the main reason that Kat had a brick in her hands, ready to smash Rome's windows out. Kat asked him not to bring Heaven to the block party, and the second Kat showed up, he was chilling with Heaven. She figured that they had to be fucking; no man could be around a woman like Heaven and not be having sex with her.

Kat was wrong, and now was making a scene. The entire hood knew how crazy Kat was, and Rome wouldn't listen. All he saw was her ass, and beautiful shape. It was enough for Rome to disregard her craziness, and Heaven was sitting back, laughing from the pits of her stomach. Rome chases her around his car, trying to snatch the brick from her. He loved his car more than anything, and he had just bought it. Rome spent his last on it, and it was typical hood shit, buying something that he couldn't afford just to look fly. Rome was fresh home from a two-year bid in prison for a gun charge. He was from a neighborhood that you needed to carry one, or you would end up a victim. Rome stopped and shrugged his shoulders. The look on Heaven's face only made him angrier; he was done playing games. He shook his head in frustration, and his high was gone now.

" Kat, please put the brick down, and come over here. I'm not playing, if you throw that brick in my car, it's going to be a problem!" Rome took his shades off from his face, and he wanted her to see how serious he was right now.

Kat acted like she was going to toss the brick at his window, and started to laugh. Everyone in the crowd watched in anticipation, knowing that she was crazy as a bat out of hell. She made have had a smile on her face, but she was serious, and God himself couldn't stop her from busting his windows out.

" You got me all the way fucked up! You got the right bitch today, I told you don't be here with this bitch, and when I get here, you all up in this bitch face laughing! You know what? I should bust this bitch in the head with this brick," Kat said, looking directly at Heaven.

" Yo! Chill!" Rome shouted.

Heaven's smiled left her face immediately, and she got on her hot girl shit. She didn't know that's why she was trying to bust Rome's windows out. She exhaled deeply and smacked her lips. Heaven giggled, and didn't understand why his girlfriend felt threatened by her. It wasn't like that between them, and no matter how many times they both said it, nobody believed them.

" You need to check your insecurities, sus! It's not even like that; I don't want your man. You just a fuck to Rome, boo-boo! I have my own man, and you out here with that bogus ass, crooked ass frontal. Stop it!" Heaven started to walked towards Kat, and Rome grabbed her. " Rome, check your, bitch! A hoe could never!"

Heaven words cut her deep, and Rome tried to lunge towards Kat, but he was too slow. The brick smacked his windshield and glass shattered everywhere, the crowd started to laugh, and the DJ cut the music. Kat took off running and stepped inside her car and drove off, never looking back. Rome tried to chase after her, but she was long gone, and he tried to catch his breath. The neighborhood fiend by the name of Twin patted Rome on his back.

" Don't worry about that shit, young blood, give me eight dollars, and let good ole Twin fix that window for you," Twin said, smiling, exposing his yellow teeth.

" Twin, not now, brah! Get your ass away from me," Rome walked back and stared at Heaven.

" What? I ain't do shit! It is not my fault that your girl thinks we fucking! I have my own man, thank you," She said. Heaven gave him the bottle of D'usse and smiled. " You weren't going to call her after tonight anyway, and she would have still bust your windows out. So, don't trip!"

" Don't trip? Look at my car, Stinky!" Rome said, calling her by her childhood nickname.

" Let's party and worry about that later," Heaven said, still holding the bottle of liquor in her hands.

Rome snatched the bottle and chuckled. " DJ, turned that fuckin' music back up!"

#

" Heaven and Rome, if you don't get y'all drunk asses out my living room!" Rome's grandmother, G-Mama, shouted. She had been kicking them out of her house since the both of them were ten years old. They both were twenty-five now, and it was the same thing; Rome and Heaven didn't even know how they ended it up at G-Mama's house. They both had drunk so much that they passed out on the couch. Heaven's phone was ringing off the hook, and she had over thirty missed calls. She was too drunk to drive home, and now her man, Reese, was losing his mind. He did not doubt in his mind who she was with, but it wasn't like that. She truly did love Reese, and didn't want to lose him. She would make fun of Rome and all the girls he would date, but she was in a real relationship, and didn't want to lose Reese. She let the liquor get the best of her, and the raspy voice of G-Mama made her realize that she wasn't at home, and was at Rome's grandmother's house.

Rome laid their still sleep, and smelled like liquor mixed with weed. He was drooling on the side of his face, and G-Mama looked at him like he was crazy. They both had their own apartments but always seemed to end up at her house. It was like they couldn't help it; G-Mama smacked Rome across his leg, waking him up from his deep sleep. He looked at his grandmother standing over him, and realized that he was most likely late. His car was parked in the driveway with a busted windshield, and he was supposed to meet his parole officer two hours ago. Rome hated going down to meet with his P.O. once every two weeks to piss in a cup. It was the worst part of his week, not to mention he had no money to get his window fixed. Rome was still figuring out what he wanted to do with his life, he was caught up in the streets, and if hadn't been for Heaven, he would be in even deeper. He needed cash, and he needed some fast, he wasn't down with being a broke nigga. He was going to come up one way or another, and he would bring his ace, Heaven with him.

He stretched his arms and legs out, he picked up his phone, and exhaled deeply. Rome looked at the time, and jumped up from off the couch. G-Mama smacked him upside his head; she expected so much more from him. Rome was a grown man now, and she was praying that he didn't end up dead messing with the streets. Rome's brother was killed a few years back, and G-Mama couldn't lose him too. Her heart wouldn't be able to take it, Rome was different, and everyone could see it. He was destined to be someone, the universe had special plans for him, and it was up to him not to fuck it up. Heaven's facial expression said it all as she listened to the voicemails Reese left her. Rome snatched the phone from her and chuckled.

" Fixed your face, Stinky! You want me to talk to that lame-ass man," Rome chuckled.

" Why would I do that? He already thinks I'm fucking you. I really like him, Rome. I might have fucked this up," Heaven said, grabbing her things. " Can you give me a ride home? I don't even feel like driving; I'm still drunk."

" If you don't mind riding with a smashed window, I got you. I have to see my parole officer anyway. I hope he doesn't lock my ass back up; I was supposed to be there hours ago. Give me ten minutes to at least changed my clothes and wash my face," Rome said.

" You really about to take a hoe bath?" Heaven laughed.

" Yup!" Rome said proudly.

G-Mama looked at them both, and she didn't understand them. It was clear that they belonged together, but they genuinely didn't look at each other in that way. It was a real friendship, and nothing more. " Y'all are so cute together, why aren't y'all dating?"

" What? Stinky? Naw, I'm good; that's my homie," Rome laughed.

" No offense, but your grandson is a hoe," Heaven said.

" None taken," Rome said, walking up the stairs.

Heaven sat back down on the couch; she brushed off what G- Mama said to her. She didn't look at Rome like that. Her phone rang again, and it was Reese, she wasn't going to pick up now, Heaven would deal with that when she got back home. She knew that she was in for war; she was starting to think that maybe her friendship with Rome was getting in the way of either of them finding true love.

#

Rome watched as Heaven slammed the door to his Mercedes, and he cringed at how hard she shut the door. No matter how many times he told her not to slam his door, she did it anyway. He placed his shades on and drove off, Rome was already late to see his P.O., and he wasn't in a rush to take a damn drug test. Rome could feel the wind smack him in the face from the huge hole in his window. It was glass all over the floor, and Rome didn't care, he would deal with that later. She turned the music up and bobbed his head as his favorite song blasted through the speakers. His phone was ringing nonstop, and he couldn't understand why Kat was still calling him. He didn't know how she could even think that they would be cool after fucking up his car. He knew then he should have listened to everyone when they said Kat was crazy. Rome tossed his phone on the passenger seat; he wasn't about to worry about it. He had bigger problems with finding work, and if he didn't find one soon, he would be back in jail. It was hard to find a job. Rome wasn't going to work at any ole place.

He wasn't about to be flipping burgers at some bullshit job for pennies, that wasn't how he operated. Rome wanted the big bucks, and getting rich was his only focus. Rome wanted to make G-Mama proud of him, she took him in after his father died in a car crash, and Rome's mother was hooked on drugs and somewhere on the streets. Losing his mother to the needle was the hardest thing he ever had to do as a kid, it hurt his soul to see his mother like that. He would see her now and then, but she would never take the help he would offer. Rome thought that if he had money that he could get her the help that she needed. But what he failed to realize that all the money in the world couldn't get his mother clean, she would have to want to get clean. It's always been G-Mama and Heaven in his corner, and that's all he needed in his mind. Rome was on his way to the top; he just didn't know it yet.

" What the fuck you looking at? You ain't never seen a busted window?" Rome shouted at the car next to him at the red light. The car filled with girls giggled at him, and Rome chuckled. He couldn't help but laugh with them; his shit was fucked up really bad. The light turned green, and he sped off, not caring about what people thought about him. Rome picked his phone back up from off the seat, and thought about calling Heaven to see if she was okay. He decided against it, and he didn't want to start more trouble. He understood that Heaven didn't want him to talk to Reese, but he was thinking about doing it anyway. If Reese could see that nothing was going on, and they were friends, maybe, he could fix things between them. Rome didn't understand that it was nothing he could tell Reese; he wasn't comfortable with them hanging out all the time. It was going to fix anything, their friendship was in danger, and neither of them saw it coming. Rome whipped his car in the parking lot, and was about to get out when Kat called again. He picked the phone up, and thought she needed to hear it from his mouth.

" Yoo! Why are you steady calling me? You bust my damn window out over nothing, this ain't going to work," Rome was yelling.

" You mad at me?" Kat said calmly. Her entire demeanor changed, and she wasn't the same person from last night. She acted as if nothing ever happened.

" Are you on drugs, Kat? Hell yeah, I'm mad! I told you that Heaven and I are friends! But nooo! You wanted to act a damn fool, and this isn't going to work. I wished you the best," Rome stepped out his car and started to walk towards the building office.

" Rome, I'm sorry. I let my girl get in my ear, but I'll get your window fixed. Please! Come to my house when you're done," Kat said.

Rome didn't have all his marbles, and all he could think about was her fat ass. He still had a lot of growing up to do even though he was a grown man.

He was attracted to crazy women, and strangely, it turned him on. " Whatever! I'll be there later."

" Okay, bae."

He placed his phone back in his pocket and walked inside the office building. He signed his name on the board and was about to sit down when his P.O. came walking from out the back. Rome cursed underneath his breath and stood back up, he tried to shake his P.O.'s hand, but he looked at it him like he was crazy.

" You're late, and you were two minutes from being violated. I'm not going to keep giving you chances, have you found a job yet?" The P.O. said.

" I haven't found one yet, but I'm working on it," Rome explained.

" It's simple, you work, or you go back to jail. You have one week, now piss in the cup!"

Rome snatched the cup and went into the back; he shook his head. It was the moment when he realized that it was going to be a long six months. That's all he had left on parole, and it felt like an eternity.

CHAPTER TWO

Heaven was still drunk from the night before, and she wasn't feeling that argument that she knew was coming the second she walked inside her apartment. Heaven had her head on straight, and wanted to start a life with Reese. She liked him that much, but the only thing was his insecurities. She understood that some of the problems she had were because of her, but all she asked was for Reese to trust her. If they didn't have that, then what was the point of being together. Heaven was a major player for a marketing firm, and her career was starting to take off. Big things were about to happen, and she hoped that he would be by her side. Heaven didn't have many friends; it was only Rome, and Jazzy. Reese always questioned her on why Heaven never hanged out with Jazzy more, but the truth was she did, he was so busy focused on Rome, that he never noticed. She knew that he was having a fit, her phone died hours ago, and Heaven had no idea who stole her charger.

She unlocked her door and walked inside, and Jazzy was sitting on her couch talking loudly on the phone. Heaven had a confused look on her face; she didn't know Jazzy was coming over. Heaven smiled at her friend as she listened to her gossip on the phone; it was what she did best. Jazzy was a hood chick, and didn't care what she said out her mouth. She was ratchet and proud of it. Heaven nodded her head and looked around her apartment, and Reese was nowhere to be found. She was kind of happy he was gone, Heaven didn't want to fight in front of Jazzy, she loved her friend, but she didn't want her business out in the street. Heaven sat down on the couch, and snatched the blunt from Jazzy's hand and took a deep pull. She leaned her head back on the sofa and blew the smoke into the air. She plugged her phone up on her spare charger, and waited for her iPhone to come back on, so she could call Reese, and see would he come back home. Heaven puffed the high-grade weed, and hoped that it would level her out.

She had drunk so much last night that it reminded her of her college days. Heaven hadn't partied like that in a while, she was busy working, and now that she had some vacation time, she wanted to spend some time with her best friend and Reese. She didn't find anything wrong with wanting to get some hood love. Heaven was trying to make everyone happy, and it was becoming stressful. She wanted to make her man happy, but she also didn't want to lose Rome's friendship. It was complicated because Rome was a man, and not a woman. If the tables were turned, it wouldn't be a problem, and that's what pissed her off. It was like men and women were incapable of being friends without it turning into something sexual. Heaven and Rome was a prime example that the world was wrong, and she wished that Reese would see that. She cared for Reese so much, that she was thinking of falling back from Rome, and work on her relationship with Reese.

Jazzy hung the phone up and shook her head at her friend. She had spent the last eight hours covering for her. Reese had been calling Jazzy for hours, asking about Heaven, and she lied to him. She told Reese that Heaven was passed out drunk, and she couldn't talk. Jazzy knew where Heaven was at, and wasn't going to throw her friend under the bus. She wasn't that type of chick, and would hold her friend down the way a real bitch would.

" Yo, what's up with you? I've been lying to your man all night, where you been? You know what, don't even answer that! You were with Rome fine ass, right? I want to give that nigga some pussy so bad," Jazzy said, seriously. She didn't care what came out of her mouth, and she spoke how she felt at all times.

" Ugggh! Rome is not that fine! I don't know why y'all be all over him! I was drunk and ended up at G-Mama's house. My phone went dead, and it was so lit out there last night. Why you didn't come, girl?" Heaven giggled.

" You know I work nights, bitch! You need to stop smiling and wipe that smirk off your face, and call Reese," Jazzy said.

" How mad was he? Did he believe you?" Heaven asked.

" He said he did, but the entire world knows you were with Rome," Jazzy said, scrolling through her phone on Instagram. " You going to lose a good man fuckin' with Rome, girl. Reese is fine and has a good job, why are you sweating Rome for? Y'all fuckin'?"

Heaven exhaled deeply and didn't understand while everyone kept saying that. " I'm not like these other hoes out here; I've been Rome's friend before all y'all thought he was fine. I remember when Rome was scared to talk to girls. That's my friend, nothing more!"

" Yeah, okay! Whatever you say!" Jazzy said, not buying whatever her friend was selling. She could see the sparkle in her eye when she talked about him. It was so obvious, and everyone saw it, but Heaven and Rome.

Heaven phone ring, and it was a FaceTime from Rome; she answered it without hesitation. " *What's up?*"

" *Yo! How did everything go? He's not mad at you, is he? Let me talk to him; I'll fix this, and I feel bad that I kept you out all night. I know how much you care about him, let me talk to him,*" Rome said. He genuinely wanted to help Heaven out, he hated to see her sad, and he wanted to see her happy with Reese.

" *He's not here, but crazy ass Jazzy is here. I'm about to call him now, I'll call you later and let you know,*" Heaven said.

" *Okay, cool! Love you, Stinky!!* Rome said playfully.

Heaven hung the phone up, and Jazzy was staring at her like she was crazy. She shrugged her shoulders and laughed. " What?"

" I love you, Stinky? Really, bitch, and why are you smiling so hard?" Jazzy asked.

" Shut up!" Heaven got up and walked in the other room, and called Reese. She wanted to say how sorry she was, and how she could make it up to him. Heaven would make it her mission to prove how much she loved him from now on.

#

Reese looked at his phone and ignored the calls that he was getting from Heaven. He knew that it was petty, and childish, but he didn't give a shit. He wanted her to feel how he felt when she stayed out all night, not picking up his calls. Reese had a deep chocolate skin complexion, with a neatly shaped goatee. His hair was cut low, with waves, and he always wore his signature gold chain with a cross. Reese was a street dude who had deep insecurities about Rome; he knew how much respect he got from the ladies in the hood, and that's what scared him. He had all the money, cars, clothes, but it couldn't compare to the love Rome got. That's what Reese wanted, and jealousy also played a massive part in why he didn't wish to have Heaven around him. He didn't give a fuck about them being childhood friends, Heaven was his lady now, and he didn't give a fuck how long they knew each other. Reese knew in his heart that she was with Rome, and Jazzy could lie all she wanted, he didn't believe a single word she said.

Heaven scoffed at her phone as she got sent to the voicemail for the sixth time. She had laid out the works for him. She was in her two-piece lingerie set, and rose petals were throughout the bathroom. She had his bath water ran, and even slaved over the stove to have his meal waiting on him. Heaven was bringing out all the stops to show him how much she cared about him. She was on her third glass of wine, and now she was starting to lose her cool. If this was how he felt last night, then Heaven got it. She was pissed, and Heaven knew precisely what Reese was doing. She knew that he was listening to his stupid ass friends and was trying to get her back. Heaven was ready to give him some of her love box, and was on a mission to put it down. She was looking like a snack, and Reese missed out on it being an asshole. This wasn't going to solve anything, and two wrongs didn't make at right.

Hours went by, and it was still no sign of Reese. All of her candles were burned out, and the food was ice cold. She was now in jogging pants with only her bra on, and now the bottle of wine was empty. She was ready to rip Reese a new one, but she was starting to worry that maybe something happened. They both made a promise that Reese wouldn't stay out past twelve with him calling to check-in. He lived a dangerous life out there on the streets; anything could happen. Reese was a mid-level dealer in hopes of being the king. He had put his work in, and shit was starting to pay off now. All types of thoughts crossed her mind; she didn't know what to believe at this point. But if he didn't show up soon, Heaven would get in her car and go looking for him. She had no problem pulling up on the block he stood out on, and see if he was okay. She jumped up from the couch, and stood up after the front door opened.

Reese walked in with one of his homies and reeked of weed. In his hands was a bag filled with McDonald's, and he was munching on a BigMac. His friend, Pug, also was stuffing his face. The look on Heaven's face was priceless, and he wasn't going to lose her cool, she understood that she was wrong for doing what she did. All she wanted now was to make up with her man, and have amazing sex. She quickly walked over to Pug and pushed him back out of her house.

" Not today, Pug! I don't know why he brought you to my house this late, he'll see you tomorrow," Heaven slammed the door in his face.

Reese kept walking, and flopped down on the couch. " So, you decided to come home tonight. The homies saw your car parked out in front of G-Mama's house, so you can tell Jazzy to stop lying for you now. Why do you like that broke ass nigga? Everyone likes this nigga. Why?"

" I didn't ask her to do that, Reese. You already know that I love you. Rome is my friend; he's family. I would never do you like that; you have to trust me, bae," Heaven sat next to him. She knocked his hat from off his head and rubbed her fingers through his hair.

Reese wanted to stay mad at her, but he couldn't. Her puppy dog eyes would get him every time, Reese cracked a smile. He looked around their apartment and saw all the stuff she did for him, and he felt like a dumb ass for being so petty. He let Rome get inside his head, and he didn't know why he felt so threatened by him. He wanted the relationship like they had; they weren't in sync with each other. He could see it, and Heaven didn't' at all. Reese could see himself marrying Heaven one day, but he just had to find a way to get Rome out the picture.

" You love me? I'm so damn stupid; you know that? You did all this for a nigga, huh?" Reese picked her up and carried her to the bedroom.

"You're my stupid man, and yes, I love you. You ain't getting none, Reese you on pussy restriction, nigga!"

Reese licked his lips and removed his shirt. He didn't care what she said; he was about to show her how much he loved her.

#

Kat looked at Rome's phone and saw that it was ringing. She hit the ignore button and frowned her face up. She wasn't about to tell him that Heaven was calling as he laid sleep on her bed. She was in competition with Heaven, and that didn't have to be the case. Rome was in a deep sleep and was damn near in a coma from the lovemaking with Kat. In his heart, he knew that Kat wasn't the one for him, and after jumping from girl to girl, Rome was tired of living that life. He would never admit it to anyone, but he wanted something stable. He had all the fun, and now that it was out of his system, he wanted something more. His life was going nowhere and fast. He was a week from being in jail if he didn't find a job. He was stressed out, and nobody would ever know it, but Heaven. She understood him, and knew Rome better than he knew his damn self. Rome knew that he was going to be rich, and he didn't know how it was going to happen yet, but he could feel it.

All he wanted was for G-Mama to be proud of him, and be able to buy her house for everything she had done for him as a kid. He wanted to do so much for his family and that including bringing Heaven with him. If he had two dollars, then that meant Heaven had half of it. He felt that it was his duty to take care of the two most important women in his life; he wouldn't be a man in his book, if he didn't do so. Kat wanted to slap the shit out of Rome as he slept; she felt stupid for giving up her goods to him. The fact that Heaven kept calling proved what she was thinking, and she didn't understand why he couldn't love her like that. She was so wrong, and could have possibly been the one for Rome, if it wasn't for how crazy she was acting towards him. Rome was looking for his queen, and it wasn't Heaven. It never even crossed his mind, not even once. He had no idea that Heaven was the one he needed; she was his other half. She gave him life, and he gave her the same thing. It was natural physics, but it would never happen because they both were to blind.

Kat was frustrated and wanted to answer his phone so badly, but she knew that it would cause more trouble. But it seemed like Kat liked trouble, because she was beyond petty, and making herself desperate. She stood up and grabbed his phone, she gently took his phone and held it up to his face unlocking it. She went to his camera and laid down next to him and started to take pictures with him lying on his chest. Kat wanted Heaven to see how good they were together, and he was her man now. She sent the pictures to Heaven and had a massive smile on her face. Kat could only imagine the look on Heaven's face, and it brought her satisfaction. Kat had no idea that it meant absolutely nothing to Heaven, and Kat wasn't the first crazy girl that she saw Rome with in his lifetime. She had been there through it all, watch them come and go because of their relationship.

The phone rang again after she sent the pictures, and Kat started to laugh. She was getting a kick out of fucking with Heaven, but she was only making a fool out of herself. She answered the phone this time; Kat couldn't help herself; she had to say something to Heaven. It was driving her crazy, and she wanted to set the record straight.

" *What's poppin', bitch? Why you always calling my man's phone? Whatever y'all had together, that shit is over. Damn, you just don't get it, do you?*" Kat sat sitting on the edge of the bed with only her bra and panties on, and she smacked her lips.

" *Girl, bye! I know he ain't send me those pictures, you are so sad. You do know he's never going to call you again, right? You gave him what he wanted, and he will move on to the next girl. Rome is not a one-woman kind of guy, and I have a man. Now put him on the phone, it's important,*" Heaven said, seriously. She was sitting in the emergency room with tears in her eyes, and didn't have time for Kat's hoodrat games. Her father had a heart attack, and she needed him to be there with her. She didn't know who else to call, and she didn't have time for this bullshit.

" *He's sleep, bitch! Don't call this phone again, hoe! He's done with you forever!*"

Rome woke up from the loud screaming that Kat was doing, and saw that she had his phone in her hands. He exhaled deeply and shook his head. He wanted to know how the fuck did Kat unlock his phone; he didn't have time for this shit. Rome jumped up from the bed and snatched his phone from Kat. He listened to Heaven bring him up to speed, and his heart felt like it was going to jump out his chest. He dropped the phone and searched for his clothes.

He couldn't believe what Heaven was telling him, he didn't know about the pictures yet, and he wouldn't care if he did know. Heaven's father had always been there for him, and he had to be there with Heaven.

" Rome, where the fuck you going? I know you not about to go running to that bitch! Lay back down, fuck her! Why are you doing me like this?" Kat smacked him across the face as hard as she could.

He stopped in his tracks and shook his head. " I'll talk to you later; I have to go! Heaven needs me!"

" Fuck that bitch, Rome! Get your ass back in bed, Rome!" Kat yelled as the door made a loud thud from Rome, slamming it behind him.

CHAPTER THREE

Heaven tapped her leg and shook nervously, sitting inside the waiting room. She couldn't imagine life without her father, and he had always been there for her as a child. When she got that call that he had a heart attack, she almost crashed her car. She was coming from picking her things up she left at G-Mama's house the other night, and that's when she got the info that her father was being rushed to the hospital. Heaven didn't think to call Reese, the first person that popped up in her head was Rome. She was waiting impatiently for him to come running into the room, and tell her that everything was going to be okay. She was there when Rome's father died in a car crash, and she didn't doubt that he would be there for her. Heaven needed her father to come through for her, and not die. She saw the pain that Rome went through losing his father, and she didn't think she would be able to handle that. She wasn't strong enough, at least that's what she thought. Heaven's hair was all over her head, and she didn't have time to put on her make-up or anything.

Every time someone walked into the waiting room, she thought it was Rome. She needed to see him, and Reese wasn't even a thought. It never crossed her mind that the only person that was on her mind was Rome. They both had created a narrative that they were only friends, and they didn't have feelings for each other in that way. It was all false; it was what they told each other to not crossed that line. They were friends first, and becoming more than that would only fuck things up. But in her time of need, the only person she wanted to be around was Rome, and it was the same way with him. She always told her father to eat better and to take care of himself, and now she was playing the guilt game. Heaven felt she could have been on him more about taking care of his health. The tears kept flowing down her head, and for the first time, she realized that she didn't tell Reese. Her phone vibrated, and it was him calling, she answered on the first ring, and she could barely get her words out as she explained to him what happened.

"*Baby, I'm on my way! Hold up, baby!*" Reese yelled into the phone. Heaven had Rome and Reese coming, and all she could do was hope that they wouldn't cause a scene. It was the biggest mistake that she could have done; Reese wasn't ready to accept Rome yet. It was a ticking time bomb waiting to explode, and the second that Reese saw Rome it would be on. Heaven stood up from the chair, and paced back and forth. She couldn't wait any longer, and she needed to know something now. She started to walk around and look for anybody that could tell her something. They kept telling her to let them do their job, but she wasn't trying to hear that shit. Heaven finally was about to sit down, and she started to pray for her father to make it. She looked up, and Rome came running into the room, she stood up and lunged into his arms. She hugged him tightly and cried inside his chest.

Rome let a tear fall down his face, and he understood her pain. He hated to see her this way; she was always so strong. He held his friend, and they both cried in each other's arms, and they both were lost in each other's presence. At that moment, things felt like it was going to be okay; Heaven hugged him tighter.

" What happened, Heaven?" Rome asked. He didn't know much about what was going on, and all he heard was she was at the hospital. That was all Rome needed to hear, she was speaking so fast, and it didn't matter what happened, he was going to be there for her.

" I don't know, Rome! I got a call saying that my father had a heart attack, and rushed down here. They are not telling me shit! I've been asking for the last hour, but they keep saying let them do their job. You think he's dead?" Heaven started to cry harder; the mere thought of her father dying was making her breath short.

" He's not dead, and your father is too stubborn to die on us like that, Heaven. He's one of the strongest men that I know. I believe that he is going to be okay, and you have to believe that too. All we can do is wait, take a seat and try to calm down," Rome sat down with her, and she leaned her head on his shoulder.

" Thank you for coming so fast. Your lil girlfriend sent me pictures of y'all, and I don't know what she was trying to prove," Heaven said.

" Don't worry about that; Kat is crazy. I want you to know, it doesn't matter where I'm at or who I'm with, you need me, and I'm there, Heaven," Rome said, leaning his head up against hers.

" And I'll be there for you no matter who I'm with or where I'm at, Rome. I promise," Heaven said, but neither of them could keep that promise. They didn't know it now, but their friendship would be tested. The unconditional love would always be there, and it would come a time when they both would have to choose, it would be either their friendship or the one they loved.

" Why is he here? You called him first," Reese asked, pulling her up from her seat.

Heaven looked at him, and didn't know what to say; she had fucked up again.

#

Rome held his composure out of respect to Heaven, and her father. He had that much love for her that he wouldn't dare cause a scene. Even though he wanted to punch Reese in the face for acting an ass about him being there. In Rome's eyes, it didn't matter who she called first, her father was fighting for his life, and Reese was caught up in his ego. He walked over and grabbed two waters out of the snack machine, and he knew how much Heaven likes to drink water when she was nervous, and he didn't know, Rome would always make fun of her for that. He came back and watched as Reese gave him a cold stare. Rome handed Heaven the water, and sat down on the opposite of the waiting room. He didn't want to hear their conversation; Rome tried to give her some space to handle things with her man. If it weren't for her, Rome would have never let Reese run his mouth like that, and it would have been a fight without a doubt.

G-Mama came walking into the waiting room next, and Heaven now had everyone that she cared about. Rome didn't know what else to do but call G-Mama; she always knew what to say to them to get them back on the right track. She stood up and hugged Rome's grandmother like she was hers, she cried in her arms. Reese had a jealous look on his face, and didn't want her to be so attached to Rome, and his family. He was being selfish and wasn't brave enough to understand the dynamics of their friendship. He was already thinking about giving her an ultimatum, and it was going to have to be him or Rome. He couldn't do it anymore and wanted Rome out of their lives. He was more worried about him then Heaven's father. Reese was ready to have his goons kill Rome, but it would never happen. Rome was big on the streets for someone who wasn't a dealer; he was bigger in the hood, then Reese could ever be.

The room was in complete silence as they waited, hours went by, and they still haven't heard anything back yet. G-Mama sat next to Rome, and she could see the look in his eyes. She knew her grandson better than he knew himself, and it was love. It was so clear; they both couldn't keep their eyes off one another. They tried so hard to lie to themselves, but it only made it more apparent, and if she could see it, then she knew Reese could too. Maybe, it was the reason he had a hateful look on his face, so G-Mama thought. Rome was starting to lose his cool, and wanted answers just as bad as Heaven. It had been entirely too long, and far as he was concerned, somebody had to know something. He started to pace back and forth. Rome stuck his head out of the room, and began to look for a nurse. Rome was done waiting, and they were going to tell him and Heaven something. Heaven looked at Reese and knew that he was going to snap on her when they were alone. She messed up big time, but that wasn't the case. Her love for him blinded Reese's selfish ways.

The doctor finally walked back into the waiting room after hours of making them. The entire room stood up and waited to hear what was going on, and out of force of habit, Rome held on to Heaven's hand. He quickly let it go, and at the moment, he realized that maybe their friendship was inappropriate. He pictured himself in Reese's shoes and for the first time, understood what he was going through.

" Heaven, it was touch and go for a second, but we were able to do emergency surgery, and he is going to be fine. Your father suffered a massive heart attack, and his lifestyle is going to have to change. We are not out of the woods just yet, but I'll let you see him for a brief moment," The doctor explained.

" Thank you, Jesus!" G-Mama yelled. " God is good, ain't he? Yes, Lord!"

" I told you it was going to work out, Stinky," Rome said, walking off into the hallway.

Reese walked behind him and grabbed him by his shoulder. " Yo, you need to leave, and stop calling her Stinky, nigga! Y'all ain't kids anymore, and that's my woman now. I can take care of her, so back the fuck up, or you gone see me, nigga! I'll have you touched, boy!"

Rome chuckled. " You can take care of her? That's why she called me first, huh? Reese you a fuckboy, and if you ever threaten me again, I'll put a hole in your head! We both know you ain't no killa! I'm going to back off, but not because of you, nigga! If you hurt her, and then you are going to see me, nigga! Big difference!"

" Stay away!" Reese shouted.

Heaven walked out into the hallway, and all she could see was Rome walking away. She didn't know what happen between the two of them, but she wanted everybody to get along. " Rome! Where are you going?"

Rome stopped and turned around. He looked at her and smiled. " You don't need me here; you got Reese. See you around, Stinky."

" What does that mean?" Heaven asked. Rome didn't answer and left the hospital. Reese wrapped her arm around her and was smiling on the inside.

" Forget about him, and she would never be able to forget him. She was his Stinky, and it would always be that way.

#

" I'm looking forward to working with you, Rome. Here's your uniform, and wearing the hat is mandatory," The manager said. Rome looked at the hat like he was crazy; it was the only job that would give him the opportunity being that he had a record. Rome was sure that he could have found a better job, but he didn't have much time, so he had to take the first available thing to him. He felt embarrassed working at a hotdog stand, and he hadn't even started yet. Rome knew that his homies would clown him, the second they saw him in his uniform. It was either this or go back to jail, and he wasn't doing that at all. Rome needed to holler at the hood, and see if they had a spot for him. He wasn't a dopeboy anymore, but Rome was seriously thinking about going back. He needed the money, and he would do things the right way this time. He would learn from his mistakes and rise to the top. Rome would play along with this bullshit job for now to avoid prison.

He could picture himself sitting on the throne; Rome had so many things he wanted to do with his life. He would usually take about those things with Heaven, but it's been three days since he left her at the hospital. She was calling him, but Rome didn't pick up. He needed space away from her, and it was the only way for either of them to have a love life. More so her then him, Heaven deserved to be happy with her man, and he wasn't going to get in the way of that. It was killing him not being able to talk to his friend; they never went more than a couple of hours without ever being able to speak to each other. Rome's thoughts were in the cloud, as the manager explained the job details. He didn't hear a single word, and he didn't give a fuck about what he was saying. Rome periodically nodded his head, and cracked at fake smiled. He wished that this shit would end soon; he never pictured his life like this.

Heaven and Rome would dream about the day that they would have matching cars, and would travel the world together. Now that he was older, all that seemed like just wishful thinking. He didn't know about her, but he believed that it would happen one day. Rome shook the manager's hand and held his uniform in his hand as he stood up. He smiled again, and walked out of the office. Once outside, he took a deep breath and looked around. He was hoping that nobody saw him; the hotdog stand was in the middle of the hood. It was located in the center of all the traffic, and it was where the parties would be at, and all the dopeboy, and fly girls would come to eat in the wee hours of the night. It was the only spot that would be open, and Rome would be there serving hotdogs, it made his head hurt thinking about it. Rome didn't drive, and decided to walk; he got love from all the people. Rome was a hood star, but he wanted more than to be only known in his hood.

Rome shook his head as he saw Twin walking up the street. He cracked a smile because he knew what was coming; he reached into his pocket and pulled out a five-dollar bill. But what he didn't see was his mother walking behind him, and the moment he saw her, his heart felt like it stopped. It had been weeks since he saw her, and he froze up.

" What's poppin, young blood? Help Twin out with a couple of dollars. I'll come by and wash that car for you, that window still fucked up? I'll tell you what, give Twin that five that's in your hands, and I'll fix the window too!" Twin said seriously. He always referred to himself in the third person.

Rome didn't say anything, and handed Twin the five-dollar bill. His mother walked with her head down in a daze. It was like she was searching the ground for something that was there, but it was nothing. She bumped right into Rome and looked up at him and kept walking like he was a stranger. He chased back up to her and stopped in front of her.

" Hey, you got a dollar?" She said.

" Mama, it's me, Rome. Where have you been, I've been looking for you," Rome said. He could see the confused look in her eye. " It's me, Rome, your son."

Rome's mother, Lisa, looked at him and frowned up her face. She pushed him out the way. " I'm not your damn, Mama, and you have the wrong lady. Do you have a dollar or not? Please don't call me your Mama, I have a boy and it ain't you."

" It's me, Mama! Look closer." Rome's voice started to crack.

Lisa took the sunglasses from her face and rubbed her hand across his cheek. " Romeo, is that you, baby?"

" Yes!" Rome shouted.

" Give me a dollar, boy! You leave you own Mama out her with no money! What kind of son are you! Fuck that money! I don't need you," Lisa shouted. She was high and wasn't in the right headspace.

" Mama, let me help you," Rome watched as his mother walked off from him. He wanted to cry, but his pride wouldn't allow him to show the streets his emotion. He shook his head, and the sound of a horn beeping at him snapped him out his trance.

Heaven was holding up traffic with a sad look on her face, and she knew what he was going through.

She knew that he needed her right now, especially after seeing that with his mother. She originally came to curse him out for not picking up her calls.

" Get in, Rome. Let's go home!" Heaven said.

Rome walked towards the car and got in; he was happy to Heaven because he needed his friend.

CHAPTER FOUR

" They want you to wear that shit, huh? I can't wait to see you in that shit," Heaven said, jokingly. She picked the uniform up and tossed it on the back seat of her car. She tried to put a smile on his face, and the one he gave her was fake. She saw that he was hurting; every time he saw his mother, it put him in a bad space. It was how Rome caught a gun charge, and he was on his way to shoot the person he saw serving his mother a dime bag of heroin. He couldn't handle seeing that, and the funny thing about it, Rome was about to sell the very thing that had his mother walking like a zombie. It didn't bother him to destroy other lives for a quick buck, but when it came to his, it was okay. It was the thinking of most of the people in the hood, Rome, wanted his chance to be the king, even if it was at the expense of his own people. Rome couldn't get the image of his mother out his mind, and he tried to shake the thoughts, but it was pointless.

Rome knew what Heaven was trying to do, and he appreciated her being there for him. But his position about their friendship didn't change; they needed space. He loved her that much, and her happiness was all that mattered to him. If that meant being with Reese, then he would support that to the fullest. He didn't know how to tell his best friend that they should take a break from each other. He looked into her eyes, and it clicked for him. For the first time in his life, Rome looked at Heaven differently. He realized that she was the love of his life. Rome would never admit that. He waited too long to wake up and smell the coffee, Heaven had a man, and she was in love with him. Rome wasn't that type of guy, and he was all over the place right now. He needed time to get his shit together; in his mind, he didn't deserve Heaven. Rome's nerves were terrible, and was dying to smoke him a blunt, but he couldn't. His P.O. was making him piss in the cup, and if he failed, it was right back to jail. He wasn't ready to risk his freedom for a high, but he would for the dollar bill.

Heaven was trying her best to break the ice, and it was something different about him. She could see a spark in her eyes when he looked at her. She could feel weird energy that she never felt before, and Heaven didn't know what it was, but it had her trippin'. She had butterflies in the pit of her stomach, and that was making her blush. She kept driving and pulled the car over in front of Rome's house. Heaven parked right behind his Mercedes, and put the car in park. It was an awkward silence, and neither of them said anything at first. Rome tried to stop thinking about his mother; he was lost on why she didn't know him. He would give anything to share a moment with her like when he was a child. When his father died, his mother lost her way, and the drugs took over her. It has been over sixteen years since then, and if she wasn't clean now, then Rome figured that she would never get clean.

Heaven tried to break the tension, and she started to joke with him again about his job at the hotdog stand. She held the uniform up in his face and teased him. This time when he laughed, she could tell that it was genuine. He snatched it from her and leaned back on the headrest.

" You got jokes, huh? They want me to wear this bullshit! I'm too fuckin' fly to be caught wearing this shit. I can't wait to get off this parole, it's holding me back," Rome said.

Heaven playfully hit him on his arm. " Shut up, and you just want to get high!"

" True!" Rome shouted. " What's up with your, pops? Is he going to be okay? I know I left right away, but it wasn't personal. I wanted to give you some space with Reese, you know."

Heaven smacked her lips. She knew that Reese was the reason that he had been giving her the cold shoulder. " He's doing good, and the first thing he said when I walked into the room was about you. He wanted you to be there; you should go see him. I love Reese, but I'll never stop being your friend. Don't ever do that to me again, Rome. We are together forever; remember the promise we made as kids. We said we would be together forever, don't do that again."

" I think that us being apart would be better. I want you to be happy, and being around me only fucks things up with Reese and you. It's time for me to step back so that you can live your life," Rome explained.

" Fuck that, Rome. I used to think that too, but these few days without you had been the worst days of my life. I need you," Heaven grabbed his hand.

Rome stared into her eyes, and he couldn't help himself. It was like their bodies were attracted to each other, and they got closer and closer until their lips locked. He kissed her passionately, and Heaven felt like she was floating on a cloud.

" Oh, shit! You want me to stop? I'm sorry, Heaven," Rome was speaking frantically.

" Don't stop, let's go inside," Heaven had a lustful look in her eyes. This was a lifetime in the making, and it would cause more trouble than it was worth. But at the moment they both said fuck a friend zone.

#

The room was filled with so much sexual tension, and it was a moment of clarity for Heaven, and Rome. They were meant to be together, and it finally clicked for both of them. Heaven and Rome both knew that deep down inside, but they thought keeping each other in the friend zone would be the best thing for both of them. Their friendship was the most important thing to them, but how long could they resist what was meant to be by the universe. Heaven laid across Rome's bed wearing nothing but her bra and panties, and she had butterflies in the pit of her stomach. She has never been more been nervous in her life, and goosebumps were forming all across her arms. Her heart was beating fast, and she didn't have Reese on her mind right now. She didn't think about what she was about to do would hurt him to his core, but she was finally doing what her heart wanted. She never meant to purposely hurt Reese, and all this kind of just happened. She always imagined how this day would be, and her pussy was throbbing in anticipation.

Rome admired her body, and licked his lips. He gently massaged every inch of her body, causing her to let out seductive moans. He wanted it to be right, and this wasn't just a fuck to Rome, and he wanted to make love to Heaven. This wasn't some chickenhead from the club, and he could see himself spending the rest of his life with her. R&B softly played in the background, and in Rome's hand was body oil. He slowly squeezed the bottle and applied it to her legs and stomach. Rome, with a grin on his face, took his time as he rubbed her body down. Rome was the ultimate tease and wanted her to crave for his touch. He removed her bra and then her panties. Rome rubbed her breast, and made her way down to her stomach, and then down to her lovebox. She started to squirm as he planted soft kisses on her pussy, he licked her clit softly. Heaven was going crazy, and she never had a man take time with her like Rome was doing. He explored every inch of her body.

Heaven arched her back and grabbed the top of his head; she couldn't take the tease anymore. Her pussy was dripping wet, and she was ready to feel him inside her. Rome licked and sucked her pussy, and Heaven loved every second. She never had a man care about pleasing her more than him, and that only made her want to taste his manhood even more. They were born eager to please the other person, which made the sex that much better. She was near her second climax, and her legs started to shake. Heaven shouted out in pure pleasure with each lick of his tongue. Her legs were spread wide, and her hands pushed his head deeper into her pussy. She pushed him from off the top of her, and he stood up, Heaven didn't hesitate to take his nine-inch dick into her mouth. It was her turn to doing the teasing as she licked the tip of his manhood. She watched it jump, and she sucked him as her life depended on it. Heaven could feel it getting harder as it was inside her mouth. She pushed him down to the bed, and Heaven got on top of him, and she bit his ear.

" I love you, Rome," Heaven said, speaking from the heart. She got up and sat on her tippy toes and bounced on his dick. Her white love cream was on his manhood, and he palms her breast, it was way wetter than any other girl that he ever been with, and Rome had to think of something else to keep from cuming. He placed her breast in his mouth, and turned her over. He grabbed the back of her hair, and he pounded her back out.

" I love you, too," Rome responded. Heaven ass jiggled, and he gave her long deep strokes. Heaven and Rome would make love three more times that night, and they were caught up in the passion, and admitting things that they would have previously denied. It was magic, and it was better than they both thought. Heaven and Rome had no idea how much their friendship was in danger now. It would be tested, and hard times were on the way. They had sex, which changed everything, and they would soon find out.

The birds started to chirp, and Heaven opened her eyes, and looked over and Rome. She realized that it wasn't Reese, and reality struck her. The emotional high they both were on had come down, and she knew then she made a huge mistake. She pushed Rome and woke him up from his sleep.

" Rome, what have we done? Oh, my God! I cheated on Reese!" Heaven got up and began to put her clothes on. She felt so embarrassed about letting her true feelings out.

" Oh, shit!" Rome was trying his best to stay away from Heaven, and he ended up sleeping with his best friend. He wanted her to be happy with Reese, and all he did was fuck that up. He didn't know what to do or say at this point. " I'm sorry, Stinky!"

" Yeah, me too!" Heaven couldn't look Rome in his eyes. She gathered all her things and headed for the door. Heaven knew that Reese was mad as fuck, and she didn't know how to make it right this time.

" Stinky! I'm sorry!" Rome repeated. Heaven walked out and slammed the door behind her. Rome covered his face with the pillow. " Fuck!"

#

It was summertime, and every day was like a movie. All the dopeboy's were out, and all it took was for one car to start the party, and the rest would follow. The block quickly got crowded, and the music began to blast, and it was over. Rome couldn't get his mind off Heaven, and what made matters even worse, it was his first day of work. The hotdog stand he was working at was open twenty-four hours, and guess who had the night shift. Rome was scared to show his face, but that was almost impossible. The hotdog stand was busy, and there Rome was with his corny uniform on with his hat strapped to his head. They all made silly jokes once they realized that it was Rome who was taking their order. All the real niggaz knew that Rome was fresh home, and he had to work there, or he would be sent back up the river. Rome took all the jokes to the chin because he knew if the shoe were on the other foot, he would do the same shit. He would love to be in the midst of the party, but he wasn't going back to jail.

His mind was only on Heaven, and he was scared to call her. He had no idea what happened with her and Reese. They both were avoiding calling each other, they both had a vulnerable moment with Rome seeing his mother, and Heaven almost losing her father to a heart attack. They had a moment of weakness and didn't know how to face each other now. Rome hoped that Heaven still wanted to be his friend, and he should have never let it get to that point. It was Rome's job to protect their friendship at all costs, and he didn't do that. He hated Reese with a passion, and wanted to fuck him up for his big mouth. But Heaven liked him for some reason, and would forever support her. Rome had bigger problems on his hands; he was eager to get out of the hood. Rome was one of the few people that knew the world was bigger than the block. He wanted to explore; he wanted to be more than just a six-digit number to the state. He would get out of it, if it were the last thing he did, and he would bring G-Mama with him.

It was time to replay her for all the things she did for him. Rome felt like he owed everybody, and it was time to pay them back. Rome wanted to by G-Mama a house one day, and the look on her face as all he needed in return. Rome stood out in front of the hotdog stand on his break, and he was hoping that he didn't run into Kat. He didn't have time for the bullshit tonight, and should have never fucked with her. His heart skipped a beat when he saw Heaven with Reese. Their eyes locked, and they both were lost in each other's presence. Rome figured that she didn't tell Reese about them having sex. He was glad that she didn't say anything because he wouldn't say anything himself. She deserves a second chance to be with him because he could tell that she loved him, so he thought. Rome saw his homie, Gotti; band knew that he was the key to him getting back in the game. Gotti was the only person he considered a friend beside Heaven. If he wanted to get some real money, then he was the person to see.

Gotti walked up and he started to laugh from the pits of his stomach. He pointed at Rome and had a massive smile on his face. He was a couple of years older than Rome, and was sort of like his big homie. Gotti always tried to keep an eye out on Rome and guide him away from the streets.

" Rome, you one funny, nigga! The hotdog stand, my nigga! You couldn't find shit else," Gotti said jokingly. He leaned up against the counter and looked up at the menu. " Give me a chilidog."

" Fuck you," Rome chuckled. " This the only thing I could get, I'm glad I ran into you. Yo, I need you to put me in the game coach," Rome said seriously.

Gotti looked around cautiously with a smile on his face; he knew how protective Heaven was about Rome. He was approached by her several times, and threatened him about putting drugs in Rome's hands. "You are trying to get me in trouble; Heaven would have my head if I gave you anything. Nah, but real shit! I do have an opportunity for you to be straight for life; we can't talk here, though. Stop by the spot, and we'll talk more about it."

" What's up, Gotti! What y'all talking about?" Heaven said with Reese by her side. She hated Gotti's guts, and tried to tell Rome that he wasn't his friend. She had to walk over even with them having an awkward thing between them. She didn't tell Reese about Rome and her. She figured that it would never happen again, so why say anything.

" Hey, Heaven. I was just leaving," Gotti said, walking off.

" Nigga, are you serious? You a fuckin' hotdog man! Oh, wow! You a fuckin' cornball, and I can't believe that you are friends with this broke ass nigga," Reese said. He couldn't wait for an opportunity to fuck with Rome.

" Reese, chill! Don't start that shit!" Heaven said.

Rome hopped over the counter and rushed Reese, but Heaven stood in between them. " I'll kill you, boy! Find you something safe to do!"

Heaven held Rome back and didn't want him to risk his freedom for some bullshit. " Rome, please! Look at me! It's me, Stinky! Relax, okay!"

Rome looked at her, and Heaven scent entered his nose, and he wanted to kiss her glossed lips. He took a deep breath and walked back around the counter. " That's your last and only pass, fuck boy!"

" Whatever hotdog, man!" Reese joked.

" Let's go! Shut your ass up! Dang!" Heaven grabbed Reese by his hand, and they walked off. Their eyes were locked on each other, and she whispered from a distance. " I'm sorry."

CHAPTER FIVE

" Bitch, you did what? Why? Was the dick good?" Jazzy asked her friend. Heaven had the biggest smile on her face, and had so much to tell her friend. She had made up her mind, and Heaven couldn't go back to Reese after that. She thought about Rome all day, and all she wanted now was to be in his arms. Heaven made up her mind, and she wanted to try being with Rome. They already had sex with each other, and it was amazing, so that wouldn't be a problem. She figured that it was worth a try; they knew everything about each other. He knew things about her that no one else knew, Rome knew her favorite food, movies, clothes, and why not give it a try. She wanted to be happy, and she was tired of living a lie, and wanted to live her truth. She didn't know how Rome felt, but she was hoping that the feeling was mutual. Jazzy listened to her friend talk and thought she was insane.

Jazzy smoked her blunt and nodded her head as Heaven talked. She was down to have her friend back no matter what she wanted to do, but Jazzy was a bad bitch, and she could see herself being with Rome because he was broke. She could be with a nigga that didn't have money, and Reese had plenty of it. He was fine as fuck, and from what Jazzy heard his dick game was proper, so he couldn't understand why she would want to leave that. That shit didn't impress Heaven, she knew the man Rome was, and she knew that if it weren't for her and G-Mama, Rome would have been the biggest dopeboy in the state. He had so much love for them that Rome stayed away from those things, but she had no idea that Rome couldn't do it anymore. He was about to stick his hand in the cookie jar, he wanted out the hood, and in his eyes, this was the only way. Heaven had a sparkle in her eyes when she talked about him, and felt so free finally admitting her feelings about him to someone.

The entire world knew what she was now saying, and wondered was she moving too fast. She was excited about a possible future with her best friend. Heaven wasn't stupid and knew that she had to make sure that she and Rome were on the same page. She knew how much of a ladies man he was, and every chick in the hood wanted a piece of Rome. He was going to be somebody, and every girl wanted to put their bid in now. Them girls didn't stand a chance when it came to Heaven, and Rome worshipped the ground that she walked on. Jazzy never saw her so happy before, and how could she not support her friend. They both were on their second blunt of the high-grade weed. Heaven was enjoying her last couple of days of her vacation because she was going back to work soon. Heaven didn't know how she was going to tell Reese, and she was confused.

She didn't know if she ever loved Reese, she thought she did, but now she didn't know. Heaven was trying to avoid hurting someone's feelings, but it was no way around that. It was going to happen, one way or another.

" I feel like he's the one for me, I've been with him every day since I was eight years old, Jazzy. I don't know a life without him, you know," Heaven stared off into space.

" Maybe that's the problem, bitch! Y'all don't have to be together every second of the day, Reese never stood a chance. All I'm saying is make sure you know what you are doing before you leave a good nigga like, Reese," Jazzy said with smoked filled lungs. She was speaking from the heart, and didn't want to see her get hurt.

" Maybe, you are right. I'm going to calm down; I think It's this weed you got me smoking," Heaven joked.

" Quick question, why does Rome call you, Stinky? I hated when he calls you that bullshit," Jazzy laughed.

" Don't worry about it, bitch!" Heaven shouted. She turned around after hearing keys jingling at the door. Reese came walking in, and he walked over, kissing the side of her face. It wasn't the same anymore, and his touch made her feel funny. Rome had made her body feel like something she never experienced before, and that's all she wanted now. He pleased her in ways that Reese could never do. Heaven's pussy got wet, even thinking about it.

" What's poppin'? What y'all two got going on?" Reese asked.

Jazzy had a silly looked on her face, and she actually felt bad for him. Heaven was about to break his heart, and she couldn't sit around and watch it. She puffed the blunt one last time and gave it to Reese. " Nothing at all! You're going to need this more than me!"

" What?" Reese said, confused.

Jazzy got up and avoided the death stare that Heaven was giving her. She patted Reese on the back and walked towards the door. " Damn, man. Keep your head up!"

Reese started to laugh and pointed his finger at the door as she walked out. " Yo, that damn girl is weird as fuck, let's catch a movie, you down?"

Heaven couldn't find it in her heart to tell him yet, and she needed to find out about how Rome felt first. But even if Rome didn't want to be with her again, their relationship was over.

#

Rome placed his sunglasses on his face and got inside his car. He was taking Gotti up on his offer, and he would go to see what he had lined up for him. He tied to keep his mind off Heaven, but that was seeming more and more like the hardest thing to do.

But he would push all his feeling to the side and focused on getting the bag; he would deal with all the other shit later. Rome spent the last hour searching the hood for his mother, but he came up short. He was still trippin that she didn't know who he was, and that was fuckin' with him. Rome was lost on what to do next, and he had so much going on in his life that he was questioning everything. He blasted the radio on his way to pick up Kat; he knew that he should have stayed away from her. But Rome figured that he and Heaven would never be together, so Kat was there only to keep his mind off Heaven. He had no idea that she was going to break up with Reese for him, if he did, then maybe he wouldn't be picking up Kat.

Lack of communication was the destruction of most relationships; sometimes, all it takes is a simple conversation that would stop things from going bad. Rome was feeling good when he opened his eyes this morning. He felt like it was the day he made himself a boss, it was in his blood, and nobody could tell him differently. He pulled his Mercedes up to Kat's house and blew the horn. Rome bobbed his head and sang the lyrics to the song, and he pushed the horn again. Kat stuck her head out the window yelling at him; she hated to be rushed. She stepped out dressed like a million bucks, and didn't have a dollar to her name. But she had the latest bag on her shoulder, and her designer clothes graced every inch of her body. Kat had all her priorities fucked up and thought a fat ass, and cute face would get her where she needed to be in life. She was so wrong, and it was going to take more than that to keep Rome around.

" Boy, don't rush me, I had to do my make-up. Where are we going anyway," Kat said, putting on her seatbelt. Rome didn't reply and drove off, still bobbing his head. He had a funny feeling in his stomach that he never felt before. It was guilt, and after sleeping with Heaven, it felt wrong to him to be with another woman. He took out his phone and sent Heaven a text that they needed to talk about what happened. He needed to know where they were in their friendship and if they were going to the next level. Rome didn't want to be out here disrespecting Heaven's name. He placed his phone back in his pocket and looked over at Kat, and immediately regretted picking her up. His mind was racing, and he needed to smoke bad; he knew that he was going to get dropped by his P.O., but he didn't give a fuck. He took the blunt from out Kat's hand, and lit it. Rome had fresh lungs, and started to cough instantly. He gripped the steering wheel tight as his eyes got watery. He pounded his chest and tried to take another puff.

Kat took selfies of herself and posted them on Snapchat, and Rome shook his head. The social media thing wasn't how he moved. He pulled up to the spot that Gotti gave him and put the car in park. He stepped out with Kat by his side and walked up to the house. He knocked on the door, and waited for someone to come and let him inside.

Rome walked in, and all he could smell was money, and he instantly started smiling. It was everywhere, and naked women stood above the tables counting. Rome never saw so much money in his life, and at that moment, he knew that he made the right decision. He walked into the back, and Rome's demeanor changed. He had steam coming out of his nostrils like a bull that sees red. Reese was sitting on the couch with a chick on his lap, and it wasn't Heaven.

" I'm glad you could make it; you are finally going to step up and be a man! You ready to get this money?" Gotti asked.

Rome pointed at Reese. " Fuck this clown doing here?"

Reese looked up and pushed the chick from off his lap. " I know this not the nigga you bringing into the family, Gotti? Naw, fuck that! This nigga ain't welcome here!"

" Both you niggaz chill! Let's get this money and whatever beef y'all have needs to be over with today!" Gotti ordered.

" Heaven knows you are here with this bitch! So, you think you are going to play my friend like that? Huh?" Rome stood toe to toe with Reese.

Gotti looked at Rome like he was crazy. He couldn't believe that Rome was doing this right now. " Rome, you going to pass up on this money for a bitch?"

Rome looked around and knew what he had to do; this was a one in a lifetime opportunity. But Heaven was his friend, and he wasn't going to play her like that. Heaven meant more to him than money. He wasn't going to get another chance to get some real money with Gotti. He thought that they were friends, but he was mistaken. Rome hit Gotti with a two-piece spicy, and he punched Gotti down to the ground.

He grabbed Gotti by his neck and lifted him from off the ground. " I should kill you right here! You a bitch! Ain't no money worth Heaven! Fuck y'all niggaz!"

Kat grabbed Rome's hand. " You going to throw this away for Heaven? Really, nigga?"

" You are a dead man," Gotti screamed, spitting blood down to the ground from his mouth.

" Gotti, you ain't no killer! Nigga, I know your mama! Play with me if you want to, and Reese, fuck you," Rome hit Reese, breaking his nose. He turned his back, walked out, leaving Kat with them. Rome cursed underneath his breath, he just missed his only opportunity, and he was out of options.

#

The power from the handgun in Rome's hand surged through his body. Rome had no business holding a gun being on parole for having one. If he were to get caught with it, Rome would be facing five years inside a prison. He figured that he didn't have a choice but to have one, Rome didn't trust Gotti, and Reese. They weren't killers, but that wouldn't stop them from sending someone at him for the stunt he pulled. Rome had no intention of going there and starting trouble, but seeing Reese there with another woman, all Rome could think about was how upset Heaven would be. He had to do something in her name, what kind of friend would he be if he didn't do something? Rome needed this gun now, and if anybody thought he would be caught slipping,' he would put a bullet in their ass. He couldn't believe that Gotti would switch up on him like that; he honestly thought that he was his friend. Rome couldn't trust anyone at this point; all he had was Heaven. She was the only one who truly cared about him and his wellbeing.

Rome had an idea that would most likely get him killed if he was to get caught. He was going to rob Reese and Gotti. All that money, and all they had was some naked chicks in there. He wouldn't usually even think about doing that to Gotti, but a line in the sand was drawn, and it was no coming back from that. Reese wouldn't take that hit to the nose and forget about it. He never realized that being best friends with Heaven would lead him down this path. But Rome realized that he loved Heaven, and he wanted to spend the rest of his life with her. He wanted to live all the promises they made each other as kids. They would have matching cars, and fly out to California to go shopping. He wanted to take her to the south of France and asked her to marry him at the bridge of love locks. It was a promise he made when he was only five years old, but in his mind, it still counted. He smiled, thinking about it, and it warmed his heart. All that mattered at this point, was giving Heaven the world. He needed to prove to her that he was done with all the different women, and he was all hers.

He sat the gun down on the bed and sat down next to it, Rome wasn't thinking clearly. He kept his gun and G-Mama's house, and he was wrong from that. But he couldn't keep it at his house, not with his P.0. popping up, searching his home all the time. Reese needed to think of a plan, and he needed to think of it fast. He wanted to strike first and ripped everything from Reese and Gotti. He never knew the two of them were so close, and Gotti knew about how Rome felt about Reese. That's what made him angrier, and made him realize that this shit had to be done. Rome stood up from the bed and was tucking the gun at his waist when Heaven walked into the room. He jumped from her coming in, and he smiled awkwardly. He could see her judging him and waved his hand, Rome knew that she was going to try and stop him, but this shit had to be done.

Heaven closed the door, and her heart started to beat fast. Rome was shirtless, and his muscular frame made her pussy wet. She was seeing him in ways that she never saw him in before, and she had to refocus her energy. Heaven snatched the gun from his waist and held it up. She shook her head, and didn't understand why he had a gun. She knew why, but the entire hood liked Rome, and she figured that he wouldn't need it.

" What the fuck you doing with this, your black ass trying to go back to jail? What's up, Rome?" Heaven said, placing the gun in her purse.

" You know why? Let's not make a big deal out of it, Stinky. I have some shit to tell you, and you might want to sit down," Rome explained.

" Nope, tell me what's going on, Rome. I've been at work all day, and I'm tired, don't play me," Heaven said with an attitude.

" Look, I'm just going to say the shit, I went to the spot to meet up with Gotti and Reese was in there with another chick all up on him and shit. But I took care of it, and I fucked him up for you. So, don't even sweat it," Rome said, trying to take his gun back out her purse, but she smacked his hand down.

" What? You saw him doing what? That motherfucka! I'm going to kill his ass, so this nigga been cheating on me all this time?" Heaven shouted.

" I mean you cheated too, and I told you about Reese, you didn't listen," Rome chuckled.

" Not now, Rome. That's not the damn point! I'll be back; I'm about to check this nigga!" Heaven walked over and kissed him. " I want us to be together. Let's give it a try. What do you say?"

" What do I say? I say that I love you, and I need my gun back," Rome said, seriously.

" We'll talk about that later," Heaven stormed out the room.

G-Mama peeked her head in the room. " What's wrong with her?"

" Her man is cheating on her," Rome ran done the stairs trying to catch Heaven, but she was already gone.

" Oh, lord. What's wrong with these damn kids? Help them, Jesus!" G-Mama looked up at the ceiling.

CHAPTER SIX

" *Real ass bitch don't give a fuck about a nigga,*" City Girl's blasted out Jazzy's speakers in her car. Jazzy whipped through the hood blocks with Heaven sitting on the passenger side seat. Heaven's face was frowned up, and Jazzy didn't know why she had to get up, and rushed over to Heaven to take her to find Reese. Heaven had cheated on him, and she was the one that was mad. Jazzy couldn't understand that one, but she was down to ride for her friend. Jazzy even brought her pepper spray, and her knife in case she had to fuck a nigga up. Jazzy was the epitome of the word ratchet, and she didn't give two fucks about what you thought of her. Jazzy was into anything that involved getting money, and she cracked credit cards, she scammed dopyboys, and did it all. That's just who Jazzy was, and she was the total opposite of Heaven, but that was her friend. She sang each lyric from the City Girl's song word for word like she wrote it herself.

Jazzy had no problem taking Heaven to find Reese, but she would have to ride with her first to make her runs. She had to make sure all her niggaz paid her, and like clockwork, Jazzy would show up at the same time every week and get a bag. She figured that if niggaz wanted to be around her, then they had to pay. Time was money, and she didn't have much time to waste fucking around with a broke nigga. Some people may call her a gold digger, and that was fine with Jazzy. It didn't bother her at all, and only the bag mattered to her. She laughed at broke bitches who talked about her behind her back, and it was mostly girls who thought she was a hoe. Jazzy laughed at women who slept with men for free, and was left with nothing but a wet ass and a high. Jazzy wasn't cut from that cloth, and they may have called her a hoe, but she wasn't a broke hoe. She would never be out here begging a nigga to take care of her kids, that wasn't how she got down. She would squeeze every penny out of these no good ass niggaz.

Heaven didn't know what she was doing, and her heart was all over the place. She shouldn't have even been mad about Reese because she had no plans of being with him anyway. Heaven was going to leave him to be with her true love, but the fact that Reese had been playing her this entire time didn't sit well with her. She cheated with Rome, but now she doesn't feel bad at all, knowing that he was doing him all along. Heaven wanted to see Reese and get the truth from him. She wanted to see his face when she asked him about what Rome told her, and if he lied to her, she wouldn't even be mad. Some things aren't meant to be, and Heaven loved Reese, but things went left fast. She always wanted Reese to be something that he wasn't, Heaven was trying to mold him into the man that she wanted, and that was Rome. She also thought that approaching him about cheating was pointless, and she should move on with her life. Either way, this would be the end, and she was okay with that. Heaven looked forward to her future with Rome, and smiled thinking about it.

Jazzy stopped the car after picking up money from two different niggaz, and this was her last stop. She had a Burkin bag stuffed with money, and Heaven nodded her head. She had to admit that Jazzy was a bad bitch, and knew how to get money. Jazzy stopped the car as a group of men stood out in front of a Range Rover, and she knew that it was Fatboy. If Jazzy were to ever settle down with a man, it would be Fatboy. Their relationship was more than just sex, and Jazzy knew that he genuinely cared about her. But Jazzy wasn't ready to open up her heart to a man again, she had been hurt so many times, and now her heart was cold.

The crowd split like the Red Sea when Jazzy stopped in the middle of this street, Fatboy said in the driver's side seat and smiled.

" What's up, Jazzy? You look absolutely beautiful today. When can I take you away and give you anything you want, you deserve that shit? I'll drop everything and everybody for you," Fatboy rubbed his hands together and showed his pearly white teeth. " Chubby niggaz, love you better!"

Jazzy smiled and couldn't help but giggled. Fatboy was the only man that give her chills and butterflies in the pit of her stomach. If she was ever to stop scamming niggaz, Fatboy was who she would be with. " Thank you, Fatboy. I'm not ready for that yet; it's this new purse out and I...."

Fatboy cut her off. " Don't even finish. I have my people bring you over twenty thousand later. I got you, Jazzy. I'll wait for you forever! Heaven, what's up? You good? Tell Jazzy I'm the man for her."

" Hey, Fatboy! You know this girl crazy; she doesn't know what's good for her," Heaven laughed.

" Love you, Fatboy, and thank you. Call me later!" Jazzy blew him a kiss and drove off.

Heaven looked at Jazzy and shook her head. " Bitch, twenty thousand? It's that easy, huh? That nigga loves the shit out of you."

" Yeah, I know. Fatboy is a good man! I'm just not ready, and maybe when I am ready, he still will be free," Jazzy said.

" Bitch, you crazy!"

#

" Bitch, we have been everywhere looking for this nigga. He knew he fucked up and let Rome see him with that bitch; just leave it alone and go home to your new man," Jazzy said with a sarcastic tone in her voice. Jazzy licked the blunt shut with her mouth, and parked the car in front of the hotdog stand. It was a slow night in the hood, and Jazzy was shocked. She couldn't help but laugh at Rome, serving people with that damn silly uniform on. She didn't get yet exactly what they shared, and it was all so foreign to her. She didn't know what real love felt like, and she judged Rome because of his lack of funds. But it was all because of choice and not because he was a broke nigga. Rome could easily get into the game. His mind was now set on robbing them blind, and they would never know what hit them. Jazzy was so busy living a life that wasn't real, and she denied love every opportunity she got.

Jazzy was afraid of ever opening her heart to a man again, she felt that pain, and made a vow never to be anyone's side piece again. She would play these men every chance she got as they did her. She felt that love was for the naïve, and she wasn't ready to go back down that road. Fatboy was the one for her, and she couldn't see it, and it was clear that he loved her. Jazzy was afraid of Fatboy, that's why she never would be around him for long. He could see the real her, and he was the only man that could get to her heart. Fatboy would give up everything to be with Jazzy, and she knew that he was the one. That part scared her even more, and she would leave that love shit to Heaven, and Rome. That wasn't her style right now, and maybe one day in the future, but it dam sure wasn't going to be right now. Jazzy finally finished rolling her blunt, and she put fire to it. She exhaled deeply and let the good weed do its job. Jazzy was disappointed that the block wasn't poppin' tonight, she needed a good time, and that seemed like it wasn't going to be tonight.

Rome saw Jazzy and Heaven parked out front and was trying his best not to go out and say something. Heaven made his heart skip a beat at just seeing her, but he felt embarrassed for her to see him like this. A part of him felt like he didn't deserve her, and he needed to get his bag up first before getting with her on that level. Rome felt that Heaven deserved the world, and he couldn't give it to her right now. He couldn't stop staring at her, and he smiled, thinking about the day he would be able to give her anything she wanted. But Heaven didn't care about the material things; she only cared about being with him. She looked up at him through the glass door, and she waved. They were like kids whenever they were around each other, and it was always all smiles. The love was evident as the blue skies in the morning, and they were destined to be together. Rome wanted to go out and kissed her; he could taste her sweet tongue now. He tried to get his mind to think about something else, but he couldn't.

His vision was blocked by Kat standing in front of the door, and he cursed underneath his breath. Rome could see Kat pointing her finger and yelling inside the car, Heaven and Jazzy were in, and he knew that it couldn't be good.

" Bitch, why are you always here where my man is at? Damn, you thirsty as fuck, and don't give me that friend shit!" Kat screamed.

" Your man?" Jazzy looked at Heaven. " Please let me fuck this girl up for you! Please, Heaven!"

Heaven laughed. She knew that her friend was always on go mode all the time. She was still down to ride, no matter the consequences. " I ain't thinking about that girl."

" Rome and Heaven are together now! Oh, you ain't know? That ain't your man, sus!" Jazzy laughed.

Kat let out a crazy laugh and tossed her drink inside the car; that was the breaking point for Heaven. She jumped out the car and rushed Kat, and snatched the wig from off Kat's head. She hit Kat in the face over and over, and the two of them exchanged blows. Heaven was too much for Kat, and started to get the best of her. She slammed Kat down to the ground and kicked her.

" Hell yeah! Fuck her up, best friend!" Jazzy yelled.

Kat's friend that she came with pushed Heaven, and that's all Jazzy needed to see, and the beast was unleashed. She rushed the other girl, and it was an all-out brawl. Jazzy and Heaven were like two heavyweight champions of the world as they kicked ass in front of the hotdog stand. Rome came running back and broke the fight up, but the police were patrolling the area, and they instantly flashed their lights.

The jumped out, and tossed Heaven and Jazzy in the back of the car. Kat got up from the ground, screaming. " Yeah, she assaulted me! Lock her ass up!"

" Lock me up! I don't care! I got your wig, though, bitch! Cheap ass shit," Jazzy yelled from the back seat, holding it up in the air.

Rome knew the officers and asked for them to be released, and it wasn't happening. He walked over to the car, and the officer let Rome talked to them. " Y'all two are crazy! Heaven, this ain't you; this is Jazzy all the way."

" She had it coming! Just come down to the station and get us out," Heaven said.

Rome shook his head and chuckled. " I'll be there!"

Jazzy laughed. " You fucked that bitch up, sus! Call Fatboy, and he'll come and get me!"

#

Fatboy jumped inside his car the second he got the call from Rome about Jazzy. He never understood why when Jazzy called, he came running. He saw the best in her, and she didn't even see it in herself. Fatboy was a smooth chubby nigga who had that Heavy D confidence, and he never had a problem with getting women because of his size. Fatboy was a born hustler, and it has been the way since he was a kid. He knew how to earn a dollar as a child, Fatboy was taught the value of a dollar at a young age. Fatboy had to work for everything he got as a kid; he would buy candy for cheap and charge a dollar at school. He wanted things that his mother and father couldn't buy, so he went out and got it himself. Fatboy had the mind to run a Fortune 500 company, but he chose the fast buck. He got involved in the streets as he got older, and it didn't take long for him to be the top dog. Fatboy had money since a teenager, and didn't know what broke felt like anymore. It was always about the dollar with him, and now all he needed was a woman to share it with now.

Jazzy put Fatboy in the friend zone when they were in high school; he had always been by her side. He knew about all the niggaz she would scam out of money, and that didn't bother him, Fatboy could see past that, and see the good in her. Fatboy was determined to make her see the value in her, and he didn't care what it took to get through to Jazzy. It was something about her that made him wanted to settle down. Fatboy could have any girl he wanted, but he didn't want a quick fuck. He wanted something unique, and that was going to be with Jazzy. His homies would always clown him for caring so much about Jazzy, and she clearly didn't feel the same way. He would shrug it off because he knew that Jazzy would be his, and it was going to take some time to get her to see how beautiful she was on the inside. Fatboy wasn't waiting on her and had plenty of chickenheads, but nothing on the level that he wanted to have with Jazzy.

Fatboy rushed down to the police station with the five hundred dollars to bond her out; the money wasn't the issue with him. He wanted her to see who was always there for her when she called. All them niggaz she fucked with didn't show up, and he was the only one there for her. He needed her to know that he was in love with her, and they could be so much more than friends. Jazzy knew that already but she was caught up in the power of the green-eyed monster. She cared more about the money than finding love. Jazzy thought that love was for suckers, she had her heart broke, and wasn't going to go through that shit again fuckin with some nigga. They said if you're looking for something, you have to look right underneath your nose. Fatboy, with his Detroit Tigers hat on low covering his eyes with his wheat Timberlands on, drove calmly. He pulled up at the same time as Rome. He stepped out of the car, and they both shook hands.

Fatboy heard all about the issues with Gotti and Reese that happened a few days ago, and was riding with Rome. That's the kind of man Rome was, and he got love from everyone. He was like Rich Porter, and the hood loved him. Fatboy also didn't like Gotti or Reese, and he would take any chance to fucked them over.

" I heard about that shit with Gotti, and if you need anything, let me know, Rome. I got you, nigga. I know you just came home, so you need money, or if you want to get into the game, I got you," Fatboy said. He meant every word and was genuinely there for him.

" I appreciate that shit; I might take you up on your offer. I have some shit I want to run by you. It's a lot of money involved for both of us," Rome said.

" I'm always down for some more money. We'll talk later, let's get these crazy-ass girls." Fatboy opened the door to the station, and posted the bond for Jazzy and Heaven. He stopped Rome from paying, and nodded his head.

Rome shook his head, and let Fatboy do his thing, and he was willing to pay for Heaven's bond. He didn't care what it cost, and if he didn't have it, then he would put his ski mask on and get his the fast way. They waited for about an hour before they brought Jazzy and Heaven out. Once he saw her, he laughed. Heaven's hair was wildly over her head, and she had a look of embarrassment on her face. She knew that she should have never let Kat get inside her head, and another part of her was happy to beat her ass finally.

Jazzy hugged Fatboy and kissed the side of his face. " I'm going to pay you back every penny, Fatboy."

" Stop that, and I don't care about the money, I care about you. That's my only concern, and you can pay me back by going on a date with me," Fatboy smiled devilishly.

Jazzy wanted to say no because she didn't want to lead him on in any way, but she couldn't, Jazzy figure that one date couldn't hurt. She didn't go off emotions, but tonight for some reason, she was glad that Fatboy was there with her. " I can do that."

Heaven kissed Rome passionately. " I love you, Rome."

" I love you too," Rome said. He would have to get used to them being more than friends, but he was so happy to be with her.

CHAPTER SEVEN

Reese placed his key inside the door, and the locks had been changed. He called himself, trying to give Heaven the time she needed to think about their relationship. The shocked look on his face spoke volumes, he knew damn well Heaven didn't change the locks, and he started to pound on the door with force. It had been three days since the last time he talked to her or seen Heaven. In his mind, he knew that Rome went back and ran his mouth, and now it was beef. Reese was seriously thinking about killing Rome. He needed him out of the way, and everything was good until he got out of jail. He knew how close they were when he first started to date Heaven, but it was cool because Rome was locked up. He didn't have to worry about him, but he always cheated on Heaven, and he never stayed out, and always came home. In his mind, it showed how much he loved her. She was his main chick, and Heaven was blinded by who he really was, but not she could see clearly.

" Heaven open this motherfuckin' door! I know you are in there," Reese had wrinkles in the middle of his forehead, and he was upset now. He could hear her moving around, and all he wanted to do was talk to her, but she was playing games. Reese instantly thought that Rome was inside, and he was about to kick the door down to see for himself. He never came this close to losing her before, and it took for him to lose her to realize how much she meant to him. It was too late now, and Reese could handle that. He kicked the door, and he could hear Heaven crying on the other side. It made him feel a certain kind of way, and it clicked in his mind. He should have treated her better, and maybe this wouldn't have happened. But this was inevitable, and she tried to convince herself that she loved Reese, and for that, she was sorry. Heaven couldn't deny the love that she had for Rome any longer. She needed someone who understood her to the fullest, and that was Rome. She did not doubt in her mind that he would ever cheat on her, Heaven could genuinely be happy now.

She stood on the other side of the door in tears, and was scared that he would do something to her. Reese had hit her once before, and she stayed. Heaven wasn't going to allow him to put his hands on her again. She grabbed her cell phone and called the police. Heaven didn't know what else to do, and wanted to move on now. She called Jazzy and didn't want to be by herself, but Reese was coming inside, and the door standing between the two of them wasn't going to stop him. He didn't know what he was going to do once he kicked it down, but he needed to talk this through with her. Every relationship had their ups and downs, and he thought that they could work this out. But it was over; there was nothing left else to say. Rome had her heart, and showed her things that Reese could never do in bed. Rome was her best friend, and she loved to be around him. She was genuinely sorry for the way things turned out, but Reese didn't give a fuck about any of that.

" Leave Reese! I don't know why you came back here! Go back to that bitch you were with the other night! I slept with Rome! I'm with him now; please leave! I'm not about to let you put your hands on me," Heaven shouted. She ran over to the window and looked out to see if the police were there yet. She screamed out when the door was kicked off the hinges, and Heaven knew that he was going to beat her. She tried to brace herself for the smack that she knew that was coming.

Reese was breathing hard, and his eyes were red. After hearing Heaven say she slept with Rome, his mind blanked out. He was going to strip everything away from Rome; he had so much hate in his heart for him. He rushed Heaven and tackled her down to the ground.

" Who dick you suckin'? Huh? You sucked that nigga dick? You gave my pussy to that, nigga?"!Reese was on top of Heaven, and she tried to get up, but he was too strong.

" Reese, get your ass off me! Move!" Heaven screamed. She was squirming, trying to free her arms from underneath his knees.

" I'm going to kill you and that nigga! That's how you do me?" Reese yelled.

" Show me your hands now!" The black police officer screamed. He pulled out his stun gun and immediately shot him. Reese's body shook on the ground from the electric surge that was in his body. The officer quickly ran and placed Reese in handcuffs.

" I love you, Heaven," Reese struggled to say, and he was still shaking. The officer pulled him up from the ground, and hauled him off to jail.

Heaven wiped the tears from her eyes, and Jazzy came running in, and she hugged her tightly. " You okay, girl?"

" Ma'am, do you want to press charges?" The officer asked.

" Uh, yeah! Fuck kind of question is that, yes, she wants to press charges," Jazzy said, speaking for her friend. Heaven sat down on the couch and the moment she realized that she would never let another man put their hands on her.

#

Rose petals were throughout Rome's house, and the lights were dim with scented candles lit. Rome spent most of the day preparing dinner for Heaven, and he wanted things to be perfect for her. It was the first time he did anything special for a woman like this, and he had butterflies in the pit of his stomach. He only wore an apron And was shirtless underneath it, Rome was oiled up, and his muscular frame would make any woman's pussy wet. His hair was neatly trimmed, and he had champagne on ice. The mood was set, and he wanted to show Heaven how much he loved her and was committed to them being in a relationship together. He didn't want her to have concerns about his past, and all the women he would be with one day, and gone the next. She made him a better man, and he wanted her to know that. He had no idea about what happened with Reese and her. She knew that they were having a date night, so she didn't want to mess that up on account of Reese.

Rome was eager to become a boss, and with Heaven, by his side, he felt unstoppable. She was always there with him, but for some reason, it felt different now. He walked all through the house and made sure that everything was perfect, and it wasn't even about the sex. He didn't care if he got some or not, and being in her presence was good enough for him. He had edible arrangements sent to his house earlier, and he was all about catering to Heaven tonight. The R&B music softly played, and he checked on the food to make sure that it was warm. His goal was to sweep her off her feet; Rome wanted Heaven to know that no man could satisfy her every need. He sat nervously with nothing on but an apron, and his naked body with a pair of timberlands on his feet. He turned his apartment into an exotic scene that was done in the most creative way possible. Nothing could ruin their evening, and all their problems they could deal with another time. It was only about making Heaven feel special.

He could hear her car door slammed out front, and he immediately went to the window to see if it was her. He grabbed two roses and held them in his hands and stood in the middle of the floor. It opened, and Heaven wasn't expecting this at all, her mouth dropped, and she immediately started to cry. But it was tears of joy; she took the rose from out of his hand and kissed his face. She couldn't believe that he would do all this for her. Heaven wasn't going to tell him about Reese and what happened, but it was so far from her mind now. She looked around and she felt a feeling that was unknown to her. He picked her up from the ground and she wrapped her arms around him. Neither of them said a single word; she let him do whatever it is that he wanted to do. He sat her down on the couch and removed her shoes, handed her a glass of champagne and fed her a strawberry. Rome began to massage her feet, and Heaven leaned her head back on the sofa. Reese wasn't on her mind anymore, and right then, she knew she made the right choice.

Breaking the friend zone between them was a big step for both of them. But now it all seemed worth it, and he knew exactly what she wanted. Heaven realized that he had been listening to her all these years. They always would talk about what a perfect date would be to her, and it was precisely what Rome was doing, and that fact that he remembered had her in la-la land.

" Rome, you didn't have to do all this," Heaven giggled. She noticed that he was completely naked, and that turned her on to the max. Rome didn't say anything, and had a smile and on his face. He led her to the bathroom and helped Heaven with the rest of her clothes. He placed her in the tub and washed her body. All Heaven could do is lean her head back, and let Rome do his thing.

" You deserve this, Heaven. I've never been more in love, you are my better half, and I wanted to show you how much I appreciate you, baby. Tonight, is about you," Rome smiled devilishly. The smiled that was on Heaven's face was the best feeling in the world to him. Heaven was the woman he wanted to spend the rest of his life with, and Rome was ready to get her a ring. He didn't need anyone else in his life, but Heaven. In his mind, it wasn't too soon, and the time was now.

" You are an incredible man, Rome. I'm speechless," Heaven couldn't stop giggling.

Rome and Heaven, laughed about old times, they ate great food for the next couple of hours. The conversation was just as good as sex, and they were enjoying the moment. Nothing could break their bond, so they thought. It was still a long road ahead of them and many hurdles to get over. But for right now, it was all about each other, and that was good enough for Heaven.

Heaven felt that it was her turned to repay Rome for what he did tonight, and now it was her turned to cater to him. She pulled him up from the sofa, and pulled him inside the room. They would go on to make love into the wee hours of the night.

#

It was early in the morning, and Rome still hadn't been to sleep, and he didn't plan on going any time soon. His mind was in deep thought, and to get to work. If he was going to rob Gotti and Reese, then he needed to have his shit together. Rome had a relationship with Gotti, and was going to give him the benefit of the doubt. He would see him one last time, and try and fix things. Rome thought that he and Gotti were friends, and for him to link up with Reese knowing he had problems with him. Gotti knew him most of his life, and he should have known that wasn't right. Rome had it all planned out, and if everything worked out, he would come out on top like a fat rat. It was his way to get the money he needed, and it would put him on top. He could do anything he wanted with that kind of cash, and he could give Heaven the life she deserved. Rome wanted to be able to provide for her, and he wanted a future for his unborn kids. The hood had a way of stripping you of your worth, and putting you in a bad place.

Rome wanted to see what was beyond the streets, and it was so much more to the small blocks that he was confined to with his peers. He wanted an opportunity to do something and make his G-Mama proud. He could start a business, and he didn't know exactly what that was yet, but he had some ideas, and taking every dollar away from Reese would be a plus. He looked down at Heaven as she lightly snores with her face deep in a pillow. It was empty champagne bottles, and rose petals everywhere. Shit was all over the floor, and the house was a complete mess, Heaven, and Rome had a ball. She never had a night of love like that before, and was completely in a daze about Rome's dick game. She already knew who he was as a person, and the sex was only a plus. She felt that Rome was the perfect match for her, and was the man she needed her entire life. They understood each other, and the most important part was they were friends first, and now nothing could keep them away from each other.

Even if things didn't work out, Heaven and Rome would remain friends, that's how deep their bond was with each other. Rome stretched his body out and tried not to wake up Heaven. He wanted to sneak out before she woke up. Rome had written a love letter and placed it next to her pillow. He wanted her to wake up and know that he loved her more than anything in the world. He smiled as he gently laid the note directly next to her. Rome needed to get this robbery out the way, and didn't have time to waste.

He knew that she would talk him out of it, and for the first time in his life, Rome didn't tell her something. He didn't want to start their relationship out with a not keeping it real with her, but he couldn't tell her, she wouldn't understand. Rome was wrong, and Heaven would understand, and would support him. That's how much she loved him, and she would forever be his ride or die. She wouldn't talk him out of anything, and Heaven would be right there, rooting her man on.

" Where are you going?" Heaven whispered, waking up from her deep sleep. She smiled and noticed the letter by her head. She grabbed it, and her heart was warmed. Heaven couldn't believe that she didn't be with Rome sooner. He remembered everything about what she told him, and it was always her just venting, but he obviously never forgot. Heaven would always tell him about her perfect man, and she would love to wake up to love letters on her pillow like in the movies.

Rome saw the innocence in her eyes, and figured how could he lie to her. He would never be able to live with himself for that, and he sat down next to her. " I'm going to rob Reese and Gotti for every penny they got. I'm going to take as much money from them and buy G-Mama a house and leave this hood for good. I'm taking you on a shopping spree, and we'll get matching cars just like we talked about. I'll start a legit business, and we'll be partners. Just like we talked about as....."

" Kids! You are serious, aren't you? You really would do all that to live out a childhood fantasy we came up with when we were nine years old, Rome," Heaven asked.

" Hell yeah! It's more than a fantasy, Heaven. It's our destiny, so please don't stop me from doing this," Rome sat down on the edge of the bed.

Heaven thought about it before she said anything. She felt like she was in a real-life romance movie, and that fact that he wanted to live out their childhood goals was amazing. Heaven kissed his face. " I'm not going to stop you, only if you let me help you. This is both our dreams, and I want to be with you right there every step of the way. You get caught; I get caught. It's either that or you don't do it, Rome. It's us forever!"

" Us forever! Let's get started then!" Rome playfully tackled her down to the bed, and she planted soft kisses all over his face. No friend zone could ever keep them from loving each other. It was far from being a perfect relationship, but they both were okay with that, whatever happens next, they were down with the outcome.

CHAPTER EIGHT

Fatboy stood in from of the mirror in his tailor-made suit, and fixed his tie. He was fly and dressed like a million bucks. He sprayed his body with his Versace cologne and made sure he was on point. Fatboy figured that it was his only chance to show Jazzy that he was serious about being with her. He could see them living their best life together, and he wanted to show her another way. Fatboy could conquer the world with a woman like Jazzy by his side, and he needed her to see how special she was to the world. Fatboy grabbed his suit jacket and placed it on with a smile on his face. His face said it all, and all his homies thought he was insane. They all knew what type of girl Jazzy was, and that was a gold digger. But he didn't care, he knew why Jazzy's heart was so cold, and he understood it. Jazzy was in love with one of his workers, and he witnessed the heartbreak firsthand. He left Jazzy on the day of the engagement party, and after that she was never the same. She lost her heart that day, and had never allowed herself to feel love again.

He thought that over time he could get her to see her worth, and she didn't need to have a cold heart. Jazzy had a kind soul, but finding out her future husband left her for a man, and was secretly gay. That hurt her so badly that she made herself a promise never to love again, and she would get these niggaz for everything they had. It was like that day Jazzy was set free in her mind, and she could do niggaz as they did her. Fatboy was one of the smoothest big guys in the world, and everyone knew it. He kept his beard neatly shaped up, and smelling good was a must. He never had a problem with getting the ladies, and it always came so naturally to him. Fatboy could have any woman he wanted, and him being rich only added on to his sex appeal. He considered himself in the category with all the legendary big fellas. He wanted Jazzy and always have, since they were young. He had no chance back then, but now he figured that he could sweep her off her feet and show her that chubby niggaz do it the best.

Fatboy stood to his feet, sparking his blunt up, and held a bottle of liquor in his hands. He checked his watch and noticed that Jazzy was running late. She was supposed to show up thirty minutes ago, and he wasn't going to sweat it. He knew how it was with women getting ready, and was giving her more time to show up. He had planned a night filled with fun at one of the most expensive restaurants in the city. Fatboy even arranged a horse and carriage ride; he was genuinely trying to show Jazzy that it was more than sex. But that's all Jazzy wanted to keep it at, and he wanted more. She wasn't ready for that type of love that Fatboy was offering; it was all fool's gold to her. Jazzy didn't take Fatboy serious, or any man for that matter. It was all broken promises and lies from men, and Fatboy was no exception in her mind. Fatboy was starting to lose his patience, and she was over an hour and thirty minutes late, and removed his suit jacket. He knew that she wasn't coming now, and he didn't like he played him. She should've never agreed to go out with him.

He kept checking his phone, and was now drunk. Fatboy wanted to know why she would play him like a sucka, and play the only guy who looked out for her. He was high and drunk now, and taking his frustration out on his people. He sent one of his men to find her, and the moment he found out, he would go and see why she was doing him like that.

" I told you not to fuck with Jazzy like that, she only cares about the money, brah," Fayboy right-hand man, Suge said.

" Fuck you, Suge! You don't understand her like I do, she's the one. I'm telling you, my nigga!" Fatboy shouted. He refuse to believe that Jazzy wasn't the woman for him.

" If you say so, but that bitch is just like all the other hoes. Cut her off and move on," Suge said seriously.

" Watch your mouth!" Fatboy said. He sat back and started to think that maybe Suge was right. He had done everything possible to show her that he was there for her, and all she did was shit on him. She didn't even have the decency to show up and tell him that she couldn't go out with him.

Suge never seen Fatboy like that before, he was caught up in Jazzy web of deceit. But she didn't do it purposely; she was always moving so fast that she didn't think about how her actions would affect the people that cared about her. The door swung open, and one of Fatboy's goons came walking in with glitter all over his face.

" Yo, fuck you been at? I've been calling you all day," Fatboy asked.

" I was down at the strip club, and my phone died. That bitch is going up early tonight, oh, I saw your girl, Jazzy in there poppin bottles," the goon said.

" What? Jazzy is down there right now! Ain't this a bitch!" Fatboy stood up in a rage.

" I told you," Suge said, rubbing it in his face.

" Go get the car, Suge! We are going down there!"

#

Jazzy tossed dollars bills in the air, and she had a massive grin on her face. She loved to be in the strip club and show her ass. Jazzy was living a fast life and needed to slow down. The only normal thing she had in her life was Heaven, and without her, she would have been up on that stage, shaking her ass for dollar bills too. Jazzy didn't want to live a life without fun, she did that once, and it cost her the joy of love. Having her heart broke did a number on her, and her confidence. She built a fortress around her heart, and she wanted to have fun at all times. She was keeping up a persona that wasn't her, and her fuck a nigga attitude was causing more unhappiness. She was hurting on the inside and she would never let the public see her suffering. She had to stay doing her thing, and with all the money she got from niggaz, Jazzy figured she didn't have to be happy. The money wouldn't be able to make her feel good, but she always told herself that it was a hell of a start. Jazzy secretly wanted what Heaven, and Rome had, but she would never admit it to herself. Jazzy figured that she wasn't that lucky to have that type of love.

She smacked the ass of the stripper that danced in front of her. Jazzy didn't purposely try and stand Fatboy up, and got caught up in the moment. She had forgotten about it even though she talked to him yesterday. She thought that he couldn't be serious, and thought Fatboy was only playing, but she was wrong. Jazzy was scared that she might like Fatboy, and she wanted to stay as far as possible away from him, and that's how she ended up in the club. She knew that being around Fatboy would make her vulnerable, and he was the only one to do that to her. Fatboy found a way to make her feel like she could be in a relationship again, and Jazzy was so afraid of being hurt that she pushed everyone away from her even Heaven sometimes. She never wanted to feel that kind of pain, so she developed this character in her head that didn't care about men. The City Girl's dropped, and that put a stamp on how she was feeling, and she took it to another level.

The club wasn't that full, but a Jazzy didn't care at all. She was having the time of her life, throwing the money that she got from her tricks. Jazzy was the ultimate scammer, and she was good at it. She didn't have to give up sex to get what she wanted, and that made her feel more like she was unstoppable. Fatboy was the only one she let taste her love box. Jazzy had so much money that she didn't want to go back to how things used to be. She was with it all, from credit card fraud to white collar crimes. Jazzy would never be a broke chick, but she had so much potential to be more, and whoever noticed that, she stayed far away from. Jazzy was tossing dollars and downing shots of Hennessy, and she never saw Fatboy walking in with his crew. Fatboy just wanted to know why, he needed an answer from Jazzy. He came and bailed her out of jail, he gave her money, and always took up for her. After all that, he still wanted her by his side.

Fatboy spotted Jazzy, and he couldn't help but smile. He was so angry for her standing him up, but seeing her all that change. He had a soft spot for Jazzy, and everyone around him could see it. In all honesty, Fatboy didn't know how much longer he could deal with her bullshit. He wasn't going to continue to chase her if she didn't want to be caught.

He would have to move on and let her go, Fatboy was a catch, and if she didn't see that, then that was her fault. He walked over and sat down next to her, and gave her a crazy look.

Jazzy saw the look on his face and it clicked in her mind. She had left him on stuck, and Jazzy didn't mean to do that. She held her head low and pushed the stripper away from her. Jazzy didn't know what to tell him, and remained silent. " Look, Fatboy, I'm not ready for that, you know. I not myself around you, and that shit scares me."

Fatboy placed his hand underneath her chin and lifted her head back up. " Don't ever have your head down around me, you could have just said you can't make it, do you see this suit, I'm looking all fly and shit."

" You do look good, Fatboy. You really do scare me, I'm not down for that love shit," Jazzy said. It was the first time she said that out loud, and she had to admit that it felt good. She giggled and couldn't even look him in his eyes.

" I scare you. Jazzy, you can't run forever. Whatever that fuck nigga did to you is his fault, I'm not him. I got you, Jazzy, and I always will with your pretty ass," Fatboy said. He knew that this was his chance, and he wasn't going to fuck it up with anger because she didn't show up. He leaned over and kissed Jazzy, she backed up some, but she couldn't deny the chemistry they had. She leaned back forward and kissed him back, and the warm sensation surged through her body. It was the feeling that she was trying to avoid, and it felt so good to her.

" Fatboy, you are something else," Jazzy giggled.

He snapped his fingers, and all types of lights flashed, and bells rang off. Several strippers rushed the floor, and his right-hand man, Suge, came in with stacks of money. " You ready to turn up with me?"

Jazzy rubbed her hands together, and nodded her head. " Oh, hell yeah!"

#

" You caught a domestic violence case, nigga?" Gotti asked. Reese walked out of the county jail with his face screwed up. He didn't have laces in his shoes, and he pulled up his pants from not having a belt. Reese had all his property in a plastic bag, and he didn't reply to Gotti. He wasn't in a joking mood right now, and all he could think about was Heaven. Spending time in a small cold cell gave him time to sit back and reflected on the error of his ways. He gave Gotti dap for coming to get him, and now all he had to do was get his woman back. Reese refused to believe that after everything they been through that it would end like this. Reese fail to realize that they were never in love, Reese was never faithful to her, and he always had different women. This was karma coming back around to bite him in the ass. He couldn't shake the thought of Heaven, and it took to lose her to understand how amazing she was to the world. He was on the top of his game, and thought he could do anything he wanted.

They both stepped inside the car, and Gotti had no remorse for turning his back on Rome. It was all about the money with him, and whatever he could make a dollar at, he would. Gotti was loyal to the dollar bill, and in his mind, he didn't owe Rome shit. He knew all about the beef with Reese, and he didn't give a shit. Gotti tried to tell him that Heaven would be his downfall, but Rome wouldn't listen. He hated Heaven for stopping Rome from becoming a street legend. He had all the potential to be on top, and Heaven always stood in the way of that. Gotti didn't know why Heaven didn't like him, it was like she didn't fuck with him without ever giving him a chance, and that's what Gotti couldn't understand. He felt that Heaven was holding him back, and the moment he shook that evil bitch, he would be the king, at least that's what he thought. Gotti thought he would outgrow that childhood bullshit love he had with her, and Rome never did. It only got stronger, and for that, Gotti was done with Rome.

Reese stared out of the window, and ripped the plastic bag open. He took his phone out and dialed Heaven's number, and then he realized that she had changed her number. Reese punched the dashboard, and Gotti looked at him like he was crazy. He figured that Heaven had to have pussy made of gold to have these two dumb ass niggaz fighting over her. But that's where Gotti was wrong, the only person fighting for Heaven was Reese because he knew that he messed up, and now he needed to get her back. Rome didn't have to fight for something that he had had since he was eight years old. He worshiped the ground Heaven walked on, and it would always be that way with him. Reese didn't know what to do from this point, and his sole mission now was to make Rome pay. If he could get him out the picture, then he could get Heaven back, but that wasn't the case. Gotti looked at Reese and exhaled deeply. It was so many women and so much money out here to get, and he looked like a sad puppy. It was nothing that money couldn't fix in his book, and he figured that Reese should know that.

Gotti pulled the car up to a red light, and Rome's mother staggered across the intersection, looking like a zombie. Reese had no idea who she was, but Gotti knew all too well. Reese was looking for a way to get Rome back, and would attack him any way he could. It was all about making him hurt, and what better way to do then his precious mother. It was a low blow, and at this point, Reese didn't give a shit. He had a new case because of this nigga; it was all fair game to him.

" Yo, look at this bitch! That's your boy's mother, she's fuckin' high as hell right now. Look at her, brah! How is it she's able to see straight, her damn eyes are closed," Gotti asked.

" My boy? Who the fuck is my boy?" Reese said, confused.

" That's Rome motherfucka mother right there, and it looks like she is going into the help center. About damn time, she's been getting high since he was a child," Gotti said. The car behind him started to blow their horns. " Okay! Okay! Shut up; I'm moving!"

" Pull over! Pull over, Gotti!" Reese jumped out of the car and ran up the street to catch back up with Lisa. She was singing softly of the song she would sing to Rome when he was a baby. She wanted to get clean for him, and finally decided to make the first step.

" Reese, what the fuck, man! We got shit to do!" Gotti shouted out the car window.

" Hey! Hey! You want to make some money, and I can use someone like you on my team. You would never have to worry about money to get high again; all you have to do is work for me," Reese gave her a hundred dollar bill.

Lisa stared at the money and then back at the help center. She wanted to get clean, but every time she was in front of the help center, something stopped her from going inside. Lisa was starting to think that maybe her life was meant to be this way. She couldn't turn down the high, and it had completely taken over her mind. She couldn't fight the urge, and she snatched the money.

" What I have to do?"

Reese smiled devilishly and nodded his head. " I'll tell you on the way."

CHAPTER NINE

Rome walked inside G-Mama's house, and his mother was sitting on the sofa, drinking a glass of water. He stopped in his tracks, and he didn't know what to do or say. Rome was planning one of the biggest robberies in his life, and didn't need to lose his focus, but seeing his mother always did something to his heart. He had a soft spot for her, and wanted to see her clean. Looking at her with her eyes barely opened, and the strange smell coming from her made him almost shed a tear. He could still remember his mother before the drugs, and he was holding on to that image of her. Rome tried to remember the good times and refuse to give up on her. He kept trying to save her, and he owed that to his father to at least try. Rome had the pressure of the world on his shoulders, so many people gave up things for him to have a good life. He was beyond eager to pay them back, and he felt like he let them down. His father died in a car crash rushing to pick him up from a pee-wee football game. If he had never made a big deal about him being at the game his father would still be alive, and his mother would be clean.

Lisa always told him that he wasn't the reason she started to use, and it wasn't his fault. But Rome couldn't let that go, and that haunted him since a child. How was he supposed to not believe that he played a major part in losing his parents? If it weren't for G-Mama, he would have been dead; Rome wanted to provide for his family. That's why Rome knew that this robbery had to be done, and it was no other way. He didn't have time to be a working man, that wasn't in his blood. He couldn't see himself struggling to work to make someone else rich. Rome felt like he had bricks in his shoes, and he couldn't move. Rome would show up once a week and cut the grass for G-Mama, he wouldn't have thought in a million years his mother would be sitting in his seat. G-Mama cut her daughter off the moment Lisa started to steal from her, and was even more shocked that she would let her inside the house. Deep down, he knew the only reason was because of him, he looked up at G-Mama, and she nodded her head.

" Hey, son. You are so handsome now. I can't believe that you are a grown man now, you almost twenty-six years old," Lisa said. She was nervous, and had been sober for the last eight hours, and it was a start for her. She knew that she wanted to see her mother and her son, but she couldn't show up high. Lisa truly wanted to get clean for her son, and get to know him. She missed the majority of his life, and wanted another chance to develop a new relationship with him. She didn't know how he would react, but she had to try. Lisa didn't remember seeing Rome a couple of days ago, and didn't know who he was, and she had no clue. She smiled, and a tear drops down her cheek, and that's the moment she knew that she had to do it for him. She had an opportunity with Reese to get all the drugs she wanted, and was supposed to be there with him now. Lisa didn't show up, and found her way to G-Mama's house.

Rome wasn't sure what to say, but he was happy to see his mother. This had completely thrown him off guard. The door opened and in came walking Heaven; he had promised her that they would do the robbery together. Rome had no plans actually to let her be involved, but he didn't want to lie to her.

" Is that Heaven? Look at you? Y'all are still best friends, huh? I always thought that y'all would end up together, how are you doing, baby?" Lisa asked. She smiled, exposing her yellow teeth.

" Uh, I'm doing fine. I'm going to wait outside for you, bae," Heaven kissed him on the side of his face, and walked back out.

G-Mama knew nothing about them being together; Rome never got around to telling her yet. " Bae?"

" I'll tell you later, G-Mama! What are you doing here, Lisa," Rome said? He stopped calling her mother a long time ago. He was down to see her and all, and wasn't going to let his emotions get in the way of his better judgment. If she wasn't going to get clean, then they had nothing to talk about.

" I'm ready to get clean, son. I wanted to see you before I check myself into the help center. It's a ninety-day program, and I want to be back in your life. I was hoping that you could do the honors and take me down there. I mean it this time, I'm serious, Romeo," Lisa said, calling him by his full name.

Rome looked at G-Mama and it was like he needed her approval. He didn't want to upset her, being that she raised him and gave up her life so that he could have one. She nodded her head with a smile on her face. Deep down, G-Mama wanted the same thing for her daughter. Lisa was her only child, and she wouldn't stop her from getting Rome's support.

" Okay, this is your last chance. If you don't do it this time, I never want to see you again. Let's go, I'll take you now and we can stop and get some food. We'll catch up for a little while, and then I'll take you in there," Rome explained.

" I would love that, son."

#

Heaven sat at her desk at work and she could barely keep her eyes open. She was on a continuous high that wouldn't go down, and she loved it to the fullest. Heaven and Rome were making love every chance they got; they both were like two wild rabbits. They couldn't keep their hands off each other, and she still didn't tell him about Reese showing up to her house and him going to jail. He had enough shit to worry about, and wasn't about to apply more pressure on him. She figured that it was done and over with now, but Heaven was so wrong. Men like Reese didn't go away that easy, his pride, and ego was hurt. He couldn't wrap his head around Heaven, moving on from him that fast without even giving him a chance. But Reese always knew that Heaven didn't love him, she thought she did, and he always told himself that he was ten times the man Rome could be. Heaven didn't get any of her work done, and she had a ton of it to do. She was the head branch manager for one of the largest banks in the world. It was far from her dream job, but it put food on the table.

She needed to get her shit together fast, her bosses from corporate were in her bank today, and if she was ever going to get that promotion, she needed to step her game up and show them that she was more than capable of doing the job. But it was nothing like the high of love, and it was the most potent drug in the world. Heaven was finding it hard to focus, and she kept texting Rome. She wanted to make sure that he was okay; Heaven knew how he felt about his mother. She had always been there for him, and now was no different. Heaven could remember when their friendship was stamped, and they became inseparable. She remembered it like yesterday, and she smiled, thinking about it.

Rome held his head low, and the tears flowed down his cheek. He watched G-Mama screamed and shout on the phone with her eyes watery. He was only eight years old, but he wasn't stupid by a long shot. G-Mama tried not to talk so loud, but she couldn't help herself. Rome knew that something was wrong with his parents, and he didn't know how to act. He heard G-Mama asked the person on the other end of the phone was his parents dead. So, whatever was going on, Rome knew that it couldn't be good. His heart rate started to increase, and he just wanted to see his mother and father. G- Mama slammed the phone down and sat down on the sofa. Rome watched from the top of the stairs and slowly walked down. G-Mama, with her head inside her palms, cried uncontrollably. Rome placed his hand on her shoulders, and G-Mama quickly wiped the tears from her eyes.

She didn't want Rome to know what was going on, but it was too late. He heard the entire conversation, and even though Rome was only a kid. He stuck his chest out and tried to be brave for G-Mama, but seeing her tear up only broke him down.

" Rome, I don't like to lie to you, and I'm going to be honest. Your mother and father were in a bad car accident. I want you to know that I will always be there for you, G-Mama will always be by your side. Your father didn't make it, he's dead, Rome. I have to go down to the hospital, and I'm going to take you next door. They're going to watch you until I find out what's going on. I need you to be strong, can you be strong for G-Mama?"

Rome started to sniff and nodded his head. G-Mama grabbed Rome by the hand and led him next door to the neighbor's house. She knocked on the door, and waited for it to open. Rome watched as G-Mama explained what happened, and he held his head low.

" Sure, I'll watch him. It's no problem, and take all the time you need," The neighbor said.

Rome walked inside and stared at the little girl standing there with a smile on her face. She walked over and grabbed his hand, and leaned her head on his shoulder. " My name is Heaven, and I will always be your friend. Everything will be fine, and I lost my father too. He was killed."

Rome looked at her, and the connection was built. " Thanks."

"Heaven! Heaven! It's some man making a huge scene, and he's yelling out your name like a mad man. The corporate bosses are getting scared," Heaven's coworker said, breaking her out her daydream. She snapped back into reality, and that's when all hell broke loose. She could see through her office window, and she placed her hand on her forehead.

" What the fuck, Reese?" Heaven jumped up from her seat and walked out of the office, and the security guard had Reese pinned up against the wall. She never thought that things would get this out of hand. Reese didn't want Heaven, and could care less about her. He thought it was love for her, but in reality, Reese didn't want Rome to have her.

" Heaven, tell these people that I'm your husband! Tell them you know me," Reese said in a drunken slur.

The corporate boss Kelly looked at Heaven with judgment. " You know this man?"

Heaven reluctantly spoke. " Yes!"

" In my office now!"

Heaven shook her head and watched them dragged Reese out the bank, and she was lost for words. She hoped that she didn't lose her job behind that bullshit.

#

Rome smiled as the small Hispanic man drove his car out of the shop. It had been weeks, and he was just now getting his window fix because of Kat's crazy-ass breaking it the night of the block party. He was surprised that he hadn't heard from her, Rome was hoping that after the fight that she would fall back from the dumb shit. He never felt so good before in his life, and Rome could get used to this feeling. He was now in a relationship with Heaven, he got his car fix, and he spent an entire day with his mother catching up. She checked herself into the help center, and they hadn't called him yet and said she left, so Rome had nothing to be angry about at the moment. Rome fixed the gun that was tucked firmly at his hip. He was risking everything by staying strapped, but had so many haters now, and they would never catch him slippin'. He would go out gun blazin' before he let Reese run down on him. Rome understood the love in the hood, but also realized that it wasn't real, and the first chance anyone had to kill him, they would. It was the way the hood was; you could be here one day and gone the next.

He stepped inside his car and blasted the music, and tossed on his shades. Rome was on his way to meet up with Gotti, and he figured that he would give his old friend one last chance to fix things. That's the type of man Rome was; he had honor. He wanted to give him one last opportunity to stop fuckin' with Reese; it would only be a matter of time before Reese turned on Gotti too. Rome sent a text message out saying he wanted to make things right between them, and Gotti sent one back agreeing to meet up. It was also another reason Rome had his gun on him; he had shot plenty of people, and wasn't scared to bust his gun. The hood knew that Rome was a shooter, and if it weren't for Heaven, he would be out here taking niggaz shit. She kept Rome under control, and she knew how to keep the beast inside him from coming out. Rome drove to Gotti spot, and couldn't help but think that it was a setup. It was a risk he was willing to take for the dead presidents. He wanted to get money with Gotti, and now take it from him. Either way, he was going to get this paper.

Rome's head bobbed up and down as Jay-Z reasonable Doubt blasted; he always would listen to the album when he was motivated to get money. It brought chills throughout his body, he continued to honk his horn and he showed love to everyone. Rome had been so busy that he hadn't shown up for his job in days. He couldn't do it anymore, and would talk with the owner. All he needed was a signature every week saying that he worked there, and if the owner could do that, then he would be good. He pulled the car up and shut the engine off, he patted his hip, making sure his gun was off safety. Rome got cold stares from Gotti goons, and he smiled. They didn't appreciate the ass whoopin he gave to Gotti last time. He wasn't worried, though, and it was only two guys standing in front of the house. He could handle that, Rome stepped up to the porch and tried to give them dap, and they looked at him like he was crazy. The world was a different place than back in the day, and not everyone wanted to be the man. Rome chuckled and kept walking, he knocked on the door and waited.

The door swung open, and Rome walked inside; he didn't even look Gotti in his eyes. Rome looked around the house with his gun, his life was going good now, and he wasn't about to get killed for some bullshit. Gotti looked at him and shrugged his shoulder, he exhaled and had a confused look on his face. He was alone and only wanted to talk. He wanted to fix things just as bad as Rome.

" Oh, so you a killer now?" Gotti asked. He stood shirtless with only some sweatpants on, and his chain dangled from his neck.

" You know dam well I will bust my gun if I have to, you fuckin with that fuck boy, Reese. You could be setting me up," Rome said. He didn't trust Gotti anymore, and he wanted to so bad, but he wasn't a fool. It was something bigger here, and he needed to know what was happening.

" That shit with Reese is more than business. He has a better connect, do you know how much money we can make? You need to stop letting that bitch get in your head; Heaven got you all fucked up. I got you, Rome. She doesn't know how to please you any way, and she could never suck that dick like I could," Gotti said. He reached for Rome's manhood with a seductive look in his eyes. Gotti had been on downlow for years, and always wanted Rome. He was jealous of Rome's relationship with Heaven, and he couldn't hide how he felt now.

Rome jumped back and, without hesitation, started to beat Gotti with the butt of the gun. He couldn't believe what just happened, and he blanked out. He kept hitting Gotti, breaking his jaw, and blood squirted on his face and all over his clothes.

" You motherfucka! I don't get down like that!" Rome screamed at the top of his lungs.

" Wait, Rome, it's not like that," Gotti mumbled.

Gotti goons ran in, and Rome started to shoot, killing them both. He was filled with so much rage, and he walked over, standing above the two goons and gave each of them two headshots. Rome ran out of the house; he jumped in his car and sped off.

CHAPTER TEN

Rome kept looking out his window with beads of sweat dripping down his forehead. It wasn't his first time busting his gun, but it was the middle of the day, and he was almost sure that someone saw him running out. He couldn't handle a murder charge, but Gotti had forced his hand. Rome had all types of thoughts going through his mind, and he should have never left Gotti alive. It all happened so fast, and it caught him off guard. Rome didn't have a choice, he had to kill them, or he would be a dead man. He never knew that Gotti was on the downlow, and that was the part he couldn't wrap his mind around. It explained why he hated Heaven so much to him, and now he was facing a murder charge. Rome hit the wall, and a huge hole was now there. He didn't play that shit, and now his only regret was not killing him. Rome placed his hands over his head and took deep breaths. Whenever Rome did a hit, it was always planned down to the second. But this was different, and was out the blue. It was a hot summer day, and a million people were standing outside. It was only a matter of time before the police came knocking down his door.

" Fuck!" He screamed out of frustration, and every five minutes he went and looked out his window. He couldn't go back to jail; they would throw him underneath the prison for the shit that he just did. Rome still held on to the gun tightly, and he didn't know what to expect. If Gotti were going to send some goons to his house, he would be ready. The universe was playing games with him; all he wanted was to be with Heaven in peace and stack his money up. He tried to get himself together, and focused. He wasn't new to this shit, and he needed to act like it. Rome knew that he had to get rid of the gun, and get him a new one. But in his mind, Gotti deserved everything that happened. He tried to grab his dick, and he wasn't going to let him think that it was okay. He didn't move like that, and he didn't know why Gotti felt the need to play him. They had been down for years, and now Rome was starting to question everything. He was lost on what to do next, so he did what he always did when he was in trouble, he called Heaven, but she didn't pick up.

The phone rang over and over, but Heaven never picked up. He had no idea what she was going through with Reese and her job. They both were going through some shit, and the love always brought them closer together. It was normal hood shit going on, and that was the problem to Rome. He wanted something different then the same blocks he rode around every day. He wanted to get out the streets more and see what the world had to offer. If he stayed, he would end up spending the rest of his life in prison. He sat down on the sofa, and stared off into space. He wanted to smoke so bad, but being on parole stopped him from doing a lot of shit. Rome said fuck it, he had caught a body, and a little weed wasn't going to hurt him. He searched around the house for some. Rome knew it had to be in here with all the smoking Jazzy did in his home with Heaven. Rome finally found a blunt, and the front door opened, and he pointed his gun with the blunt dangling from his mouth.

Heaven stopped in her tracks, and she had a box in her hand with her stuff from work. She didn't have a job anymore, the corporate bosses didn't like what went down, and they ripped Heaven a new one. She took the verbal abuse until the phrase " You people" came out of the bosses' mouths. She couldn't allow herself to work for a racist corporation, so she quit.

" Rome, what the hell? What did you do?" Heaven asked.

" I had to, babe! I had to kill them niggaz, it was either them or me, and I chose me," Rome said, talking fast. He could barely get his words out, and wouldn't put his gun down. He would protect his family, and if it meant killing, then he was okay with that.

" You killed who?" Heaven looked around and dropped the box. She shut the door and could see that he wasn't right and ready to kill again. " Give me the gun, Rome. You have to get rid of it, bae."

" That bitch ass nigga, Gotti! I had to shoot his goons," Rome shouted.

Heaven grabbed a towel from out the bathroom and wrapped the gun up in it. She wiped the fingerprints off and placed it in her purse. " Wash your hands and arms with bleach and soap now, Rome. You have to get the gun powder off, and I'll take care of the gun. I got you, bae! Us forever, okay!"

Rome did what she told him to do, and he sat back down on the sofa. He calmed down and saw the box lying on the floor with her shit from work. " What happened? They fired you or something?"

" I quit! Don't worry about that now, you stay in this house and don't leave or use the phone. I'll be back, Rome. I will fill you in later about the job shit," Heaven said, walking out the house. She was a rider, and holding Rome down was mandatory.

#

Jazzy sat on the passenger side seat of Fatboy's Range Rover, and she smoked her blunt. She had been with him since the day at the club, and she was still on edge about being around him. She was fearful of what would happen, and Jazzy couldn't help but like Fatboy. His big boy swag was off the chain, and she didn't have to put on an act for him. He loved her before she put on the makeup and all the fly designer clothes. Jazzy couldn't help but open up her heart to him no matter how bad she didn't want to, and she didn't want to even be around him. She was falling for Fatboy, and it was happening fast. It was always love there, but she blocked out all her feelings. Jazzy was sitting on the right hand of the throne, and she was taking care of business better than any soldier Fatboy had. It all came so naturally to Jazzy, but Fatboy didn't want that for her, and the more time he spent with her, Fatboy wanted to leave the country, and relax. He had all the money in the world, and never been out of the state. Fatboy was afraid to fly on planes, and with Jazzy with him, he would go to the ends of the earth with her.

Fatboy cut all his side chicks off, and didn't answer his phone for any of them. If it wasn't Jazzy, then it was no need even to pick up. He looked over at her, and she started to blush. But all that changed when she saw his facial expression; it was a look that she never saw before. He knew that he was getting through to her heart, and that's all he ever wanted. Fatboy reached for his gun when he saw a car speed up behind him, and he quickly gripped it tightly. He was ready to start blasting, but he saw that it was Heaven. He placed the gun down, and looked at Jazzy. He could tell that something wasn't right, and Jazzy jumped out of the car. Heaven was crying, and she was holding on tight to the purse with the gun she took from Rome. She didn't know where else to go and knew that Jazzy would know what to do. Heaven was taking a considerable risk riding around with a gun back that was used to kill two of Gotti's goons. She had lost her job because of her racist bosses, and Reese. She was on edge, and thought about going to G-Mama's house, but decided against it.

Heaven jumped in the back seat, and she started to tell Jazzy what happened. She knew that she could trust them with what she was about to say to them. Fatboy listened, and he shook his head with a smile on his face. He heard about what happened to Gotti and his people earlier, and he never thought it was Rome. He always heard about how Rome used to get down, but he didn't know that he still had it in him. Jazzy couldn't believe what her best friend was telling her, and she couldn't believe that Rome caught a body. He was fresh home off a gun case, and the entire hood knew about what happened to Gotti. It wouldn't be long before Gotti came looking for Rome. Fatboy had heard enough to know that he was riding with Rome, and nobody would lay a finger on him. Rome didn't need help, and he could take care of himself. Heaven showed Jazzy the gun wrapped up in the towel, and Fatboy took it from her. He reached underneath the seat and handed her a clean gun because he was going to need it.

Heaven took it, and at the moment she became a rider, and couldn't wait to rob Reese blind. Deep down, she knew that he played a part in all this bullshit. She needed to slow down, and so did Rome. She wasn't about to let the hood consumed them because it could without them even knowing.

" Calm down, I got you, bitch! Rome is family," Jazzy said seriously.

Fatboy chimed in. " I got him, that pussy ass nigga had that coming to him anyway. Rome is my homie, and the streets are going to hold him down. He's good, so don't even worry about it, Rome's got him a good one, I see."

" That's my soulmate; I'll do anything for him," Heaven said.

" That's my, bitch!" Jazzy giggled.

Heaven had a confused look in her eyes, and it clicked in her mind. She was moving so fast that she didn't even notice, that Fatboy and her were friendly. They had on matching outfits, and it was a confident glare in her eyes that she had never seen before. It took some time for it to register to her, but it was clear, Jazzy and Fatboy were finally together.

" Wait, hold the fuck up! Y'all fuckin'? Well, I mean y'all been doing that, but it looks like y'all said fuck that friend zone shit! Ayee, yes, bitch, yes! Do your shit!" Heaven said, laughing.

" It's not like that, so stop it. Fatboy is cool as shit, and we're moving slow. He understands what I been through, and he's willing to wait with me. I fuck with him for that," Jazzy leaned over and kissed the side of his face.

" I'm happy for y'all! Don't play my friend, Fatboy. You already know that we will pull up on your ass and get shit shaking," Heaven said, playfully.

" Yeah, I know. Don't y'all got court dates for assault? Y'all need to fall back on beating bitches up," Fatboy chuckled.

" Damn, I forgot about that, shut up, Fatboy! She had it coming, and these hoes need to know who not to play with, period!" Heaven said with a massive smile on her face. She had lost her job, and Rome caught a body, and she was able to smile through it all. She was a strong black woman, and she had a strong black man by her side; that was what she needed.

#

Fatboy spent the next couple of hours getting rid of the gun for Rome. But his mind was only on Jazzy, and he hated when she left him. He wanted to be around her all the time, and the love was fresh. He couldn't get the image of her smile from out his head. It made him chuckle thinking about it, he didn't give a fuck what his friends said, Jazzy was the one for him, and if you didn't like that, you could get the fuck from around him. Fatboy was also picking up his money from his spots. But now he was on his way to see Rome, and have a man talk with him. Fatboy was throwing a huge party on the block, and he wanted Rome to be good. But more importantly, he wanted to know what Rome's plan was, he knew him well, and he had to have something up his sleeve, and Fatboy wanted in the scam. He understood a man like Rome, and knew how calculated and smart he was with getting money. It true when they say great minds think alike, and Fatboy was having the same thoughts as Rome.

He texted Rome, and he had him come up to the hotdog spot; Rome had to show up, and if he didn't, it would make things look suspicious. He got a call from his boss that his P.O. came up there looking for him, so Rome had to show up, or it would be back to prison. Fatboy pulled up in front of the hotdog spot and shut the engine off to his truck. He pulled out his phone and sent Jazzy out a text. He wanted to tell her that he missed her, and to his surprise, a text came back from her saying that she missed him too. He didn't think that she would respond; he was slowly breaking the wall down around her heart. Fatboy could imagine spending the rest of his life with Jazzy, and have some kids running around. That meant a lot to him; Fatboy was more than a boss. He had dreams, and had shit he wanted to do with his life besides sell dope. The money was good, but when was it going to be enough before his luck ran out. Fatboy always thought about that, and he wasn't going to be the one who gets killed by his own people for nothing.

The hotdog stand was empty, and he didn't see Rome at all. Fatboy wasn't about to sit around a wait, and he didn't like to be in one spot for too long. He didn't even like going to the movies, and it was a threat to his life in his book. Being in one place for two hours gave the haters time to planned to kill you. Fatboy thought outside the box, and it was the way he moved. He was minutes from getting up with Rome another time, when he saw his car pull up. Fatboy couldn't help but laugh at the uniform Rome had on, and knew that he would be in jail if it were him. He couldn't wear that shit for anybody, Fatboy started to laugh harder. Rome saw the truck, and he casually walked over, and stepped inside. He gave Fatboy dap and leaned back on the headrest. He knew what he did for him, and he had mad respect for Fatboy for looking out for him. Rome didn't feel remorse for what he did, and would pull the trigger again, if it came down to it.

Rome knew that he shouldn't be smoking, but he didn't give a fuck. He needed something to get the edge off, and relax his nerves. He snatched the blunt from Fatboy, he took a deep pull and blew the smoke into the air. He instantly felt it kick in, and he smiled.

" Thanks for taking care of that for me. Do you know this nigga made a pass on me, my nigga! I couldn't let that shit slide, and I beat the fuck out of that man. His goons came in, and I had to do what I do, you know," Rome said with smoked filled lungs.

" He made a pass at you?" Fatboy almost spits his water from his mouth. The entire hood knew that Gotti was downlow, and had slept with most of his team. Fatboy wasn't surprised at all, and he heard all the rumors like everyone else. " Yo, you didn't know? That rumor had been floating around for years, and he tried to get you, huh?"

" That shit not funny; he used to be my friend. That shit hurts that he would turn on me for Reese, that shit is cold," Rome puffed the blunt again.

" He was never your friend, my nigga! He used you all these years, didn't you catch a gun case for him? Not once did he hold you down, Fuck him! He's weak now, and I think we should rob that motherfucka!" Fatboy shouted. " I know that's what you are going to do anyway, and I can help you."

" How'd you know? I am going to get that motherfucka and Reese. I want them to be broke after I'm done. If we do this, I have to be in charge, and we do this my way," Rome explained.

" I wouldn't have it any other way, my nigga!" Fatboy said. He could feel the money in his hands as it started to itch.

" I got to go, my shift is about to start," Rome said, stepping out the car.

" Yo, you look like a damn fool, you do know that, right?" Fatboy laughed.

" Man, fuck you!" Rome chuckled. He walked inside the hotdog stand, and knew that this would be the last time he showed up. He wasn't going to waste any more time in this bullshit ass job.

CHAPTER ELEVEN

Kat looked over as Gotti's right-hand man Bugs as he slept. She couldn't stop thinking about Rome, but the money couldn't stop, and she had to get hers the best way she knew how. She would have loved to have been with Rome, but Heaven was standing in her way, and she wasn't about to compete with her. If Rome wanted to be with her, then so be it, she would scam these niggaz out every penny. Kat was having an identity crisis; she wanted to be like Jazzy, and was jealous of Heaven. Those two women had her world upside down, and she was about to get herself in trouble, trying to be something that she wasn't. She had been planning and plotting against Bugs for weeks, even when she was with Rome. She loved him, but Rome didn't have the money, and that was a huge problem with her. He had the dick game, and Kat couldn't eat of good sex. She was moving recklessly, and it was all about to catch up with her. Kat was caught up in a Meagan Thee Stallion song, and had no idea that was just entertainment. It wasn't real, but in her mind, it was all about the money and saying fuck a nigga.

She snuck her way out of the bed without waking Bugs up. Kat had gotten him nice and drunk and give him some of her lovebox. Bugs was out cold, so she thought. She searched throughout his room and took the money that was in his pants. It was no more than four thousand dollars cash, and that was enough for her. She kept searching, hoping to find more, and was thinking that he wouldn't remember a single thing once he woke up. She didn't see anything else, but then something caught her eye. The green-eyed monster had control of her, and was hoping that if Rome saw that she was a boss bitch like Heaven, he would come back to her. She saw more money inside a drawer, and it was like she hit the jackpot. It was so much that she just started to stuff her bag with money quietly. Kat wasn't thinking straight, but she couldn't help but try and take it all. He would, for sure, know that he had been robbed, but like most people, Kat got greedy. She had tried to hurry so that she could get the hell out of dodge.

" Bitch, what the fuck you are doing? You robbing me?" Bugs said, waking up from his deep sleep. He sat up in the bed, and had a shocked look on his face. Kat was caught with her hand in the cookie jar, and had the dumbest look on her face. She immediately started to cry, and Kat knew that she had fucked up badly. She had tried to play it off, but that didn't work. Bugs jumped up from the bed and snatched the bag from out her hands. All the money fell to the floor, and she couldn't say or do anything to get her out of this jam that she was in now. Bugs couldn't help but chuckle, he smacked her across the face and kept striking her until her nose started to bleed all across the floor. Kat was balled up on the floor and took the blows that he was giving her. Kat didn't think that she would survive this, and started to pray. But God couldn't get her out of this situation, she screamed out in pain, but it only made him hit her harder.

Bugs beat her until his arms got tired, and he was having fun. He had killed niggaz on the streets for less, so this would be a piece of cake for him. It's was two things in the world that Bugs hated, and that was a liar, and a motherfuckin' thief. He tried to catch his breath and snatched Kat up by her neck and smiled as blood dripped from her lip.

" Why would you think it's okay to rob me? Have you lost your damn mind? Are you crazy, do you know who I am?" Bugs shouted.

" Bugs, please! I'm sorry, I don't know what I was thinking! Please! I'm sorry," Kat said, pleading for her life. She didn't want to go out this way, and was begging that he didn't kill her. She knew exactly what happened to girls who stole from men like Bugs.

Bugs goons came running in the room to tell him about what happened with Gotti. He had been so caught up with Kat that Bugs had his phone turned off, and had no idea that Rome almost killed his homie. He dropped Kat, and her body hit the wooden floor hard.

" Bugs, we have a problem. That nigga Rome killed two of our people, and almost killed Gotti. We have been calling you all night, and he thought that he got you too. We have to go!" The goon said.

Bugs was breathing heavily and looked down at Kat, and smiled. " Are you fuckin' serious? Let me take care of this thieve ass bitch first, give me your gun," Bugs held his hand out.

" Nooo! Nooo! I can help you! I can help you! I can get you Rome! I know everything! Please don't kill me!" Kat screamed. She had to find a way to get out of Bugs' house alive, and if that meant giving up Rome, then so be it.

Bugs lowered his gun, and smiled devilishly. " Oh, really! I want to know everything, and you just saved your life, bitch!"

Kat leaned her head back and started to thank god. She was seconds away from being killed, and now she had to help set up the one person that she wanted to be with, but in her mind, what other choices did she have.

#

Rome was about to walk out of his house and leaned down to kiss Heaven as she sept. He tucked his gun at his waist and tried to look himself in the mirror, and he didn't like what he saw. He was being pulled back deep into the streets, and all he wanted was to love Heaven. Rome didn't want all the extra shit that came with the hood, and he wasn't going to let that define who he was as a person. He could remember being a kid alongside Heaven, and they had so many dreams and aspirations. Rome couldn't believe that he waited so long to see what was right in front of his face the entire time. But a part of him was thinking that not being together was the best thing for everyone involved. He caused so much pain in Heaven's life since they both stop being friends, and took things to the next level. He admired how beautiful she was as she slept, and the lust bug was poppin up in his head. His dick started to grow inside his pants, and Rome was supposed to be at G-Mama's house to take her to church. But something was telling him to stay with his queen.

That someone was his second head, and Rome licked his lips. It made him happy to please Heaven, and he took his jacket back off. He sat on the edge of the bed and gently rubbed his hands across her legs. He made his way up to her stomach and then her breast. Heaven was sleep, and it wasn't long before she woke up to his touch. Rome pulled her panties to the side, and started to lick her clit. He loved the sweet taste of her nectar, and he ate her pussy like fresh fruit. Heaven moaned seductively, and arched her back. She never woke up to head before, and her body tensed up instantly. She grabbed the pillow and covered her face with it, and tried to push her body away from him. Rome grabbed her and pulled her body back towards him, and he chuckled. He spread her pussy lips apart, and sucked her clit. He had the magic tongue, and seeing her squirm made him go harder. She grabbed the top of his head and pushed his face deeper into her pussy. She could feel her legs shaking uncontrollably, and her love juice was all over Rome's mouth.

Rome took off his shirt and then his pants. He stroked his dick, and sat back, admiring her body. Heaven tried to take her panties off, but Rome stopped her, and he wanted her to keep them on while he gave her deep strokes. She bent over, and he slid them to the side, and she was so wet that it dripped down the side of her leg. He placed his hands on each side of her hips, and he slowly started to fuck her. Rome loved to tease Heaven; the facial expressions she gave him were priceless. Rome was done playing with her and started to provide her with the devil dick strokes that she loved from him so much. The temperature in the room began to increase, and they were completely naked, and their bodies collided with each other. They rolled all over the place, and made their way from the bed down to the floor, and then to the bathroom only to end up in the living room.

Heaven pushes him down to the sofa, and she hopped on his dick, and Rome grabbed her hair. She bounced on his manhood, and Rome leaned his head back. They had wild early morning sex, and she loved it when Rome woke her up out her sleep with it. Rome squeezed her nibble and with a silly grin on his face, and he was about to reach his climax. The moment was ruined, and the front door to his home opened. G-Mama walked in, and she quickly closed her eyes. She had a spare key and only used it for emergencies.

" Jesus! What the hell is going on?" G-Mama said.

Heaven and Rome took off running into the room, covering their bodies up. " G-Mama, what are you doing here? How did you even get here," Rome yelled from his bedroom?

Heaven felt so ashamed, she went into the bathroom and placed on her clothes. "She has a key?"

" I got an Uber here, you were late, and I got worried. You know it's Sunday, and you have to take me to church," G-Mama said.

" If you took an Uber here, why you ain't just take it to the church, G-Mama," Rome said, confused. He walked back into the room, fully dressed, and sat down.

" Are you listening, boy! I thought something was wrong, so I came over! Hell, but now I see you are in here sinning! I'm late for church messing around with you, come on, boy!" G-Mama shouted.

Rome didn't understand her logic, but that was his G-Mama, and he wasn't going to question her. He started to laugh, and shake his head. She could have taken the Uber to church, but he was happy that she was worried about him. He needed a good laugh, and he could always depend on G-Mama for one. " Okay, let's get you to church."

" Heaven, I hope to see your fast ass at dinner tonight," G-Mama stood up. " I'll be waiting in the car."

Heaven waited until she heard the door slam and cane back out. She playfully hit him on his shoulder. " Did that just happen, Rome? Oh, my god!"

" Yup! It's all good, relax!" Rome chuckled.

" Whatever, I'm getting them damn locks changed!"

#

Kat's face was swollen, and she had bruises all over her body. She was sore, and been up all night crying. She said what she had to for her to get out alive, or Bugs would have killed her. She stood in front of Rome's door, confused and lost on what she should do. Kat was here to warmed Rome about Bugs, and he should be afraid for his life. All this nonsense was over nothing, and you could lose your life over something so simple in the hood. She was going back, and forward with herself if she should even say anything. She had no way of knowing how they would react; all she ever tried to do was love Rome. She finally realized that he didn't care for her the same way, Kat saw the way that he looked at Heaven, and she would never have that with him. She was past that now, and didn't want him to be killed. Kat didn't wish death on Rome, and wouldn't be able to live with herself if he died, and she could have said something to help him. Kat was nervous because she had so many emotions wrapped up in the situation. She felt like Rome played her even though he kept it real with her since the beginning.

She had to admit that it was only sex with the two of them, but Kat never thought that she would have feelings for him. She was trying to get the strength to knock on the door. Kat was thinking about leaving and letting things play out. She made a promise to deliver Rome to them, and she would be the one to set him up. But it was a promise that she couldn't keep, and she would have said anything to get out there. Kat let greed take control of her, and if it weren't for that, she wouldn't even be in this predicament. She could smell the weed coming from underneath the door, and she could hear Jazzy's voice. That alone scared the hell out of her, and she didn't want that smoke with Jazzy. She didn't come on some bullshit, only to save Rome. That was all that mattered because even though the possibility of them being together was over, she couldn't let Bugs make her set him up. Kat took a deep breath and knocked on the door.

Kat was about to walk off and forget the entire thing. She would catch up with him somewhere else. She didn't come here to fight, and that's precisely what Jazzy would want to do the second she saw her, and Kat understood that. Her heart dropped when the front door opened, and Heaven opened the door. Both of their facial expressions spoke volumes, and neither one of them had to say a single word. They both knew what the other was thinking, Heaven, looked at Kat, and exhaled deeply. She didn't have time for this shit with her today, and Heaven already had one case for assault against her. It was the only reason she didn't lunge toward her and snatch her damn wig off and beat her with it. Heaven wasn't going back to jail for her, and today wasn't going to be that day. She was trying to figure out why she was at her man's house; it didn't make sense to her. Heaven figures that she didn't get it at all, and was starting to feel sorry for her.

Jazzy with her blunt in her hands, and was singing the lyrics to Megan Thee Stallion's new song. She came to see who was at the door and the second she saw her Kat, her eyes became red. She was a different type of beast then Heaven, and didn't give a fuck about her case. She lunges towards Kat, and grabbed her by the neck, pushing her against the wall.

" You motherfucka! Why you here, bitch! Huh?" Jazzy said.

Kat smacked her hand down and pushed her away. She didn't come to fight, but she wasn't going to let Jazzy treat her like a damn child. " Bitch, get your damn hands off me, I'm not here on that."

" What your bobblehead ass want? Why you always showing up wherever you think Rome's at, Kat?" Heaven asked.

" Look, I get it. He chose you; I get that shit now, trust me. I'm here because Bugs is going to kill him. He wanted to use me to set Rome up, so where is he? I only want to warm him," Kat said. She tried to walk in, but Jazzy pushed her forehead, causing her to move back.

" Aht! Fuck is you going bobblehead, back up!" Jazzy shouted.

" I'm not going to be too many bobbleheads, hoe! I came here to warn him, so you can stop with the slander. I'm not trying to take her man. Okay, already! But if you don't do something to protect him, they will kill him. I did my part; you can do whatever you want with the info, stupid bitch," Kat said, storming off.

" Bitch, you better not show up to court, hoe!" Jazzy yelled. She shut the door and took a deep breath. She hated Kat, and she made her skin crawl. " You can't believe shit that girl says. She's playing games, Heaven," Jazzy lit her blunt back up.

" She's telling the truth. We all knew this already, though. Rome is going to be fine, and he has the entire hood behind him. This has to end, and I know how to end it. I have to talk to Reese. All this is because of him, and he's the only one that can fix it. I will go talk to him," Heaven explained.

" You think he will listen?" Jazzy asked.

" I hope so, Jazzy. I really do!" Heaven said, thinking heavy about it.

CHAPTER TWELVE

Heaven walked up the stairs to where Reese hangout was, and she knew exactly where to find him. She wasn't sure if this was the right thing to do, but what else was Heaven supposed to do. Reese and Heaven were once in love, and for it to all end on a bad note like that left a sour taste in her mouth. She was almost sure that he would try and fight her. His pride was hurt, and Heaven got why he was upset. But she needed Reese to understand her position, and he had been cheating on her all this time. She wasn't here to try and fix their relationship, and didn't care if she ever saw him again; she had a bigger purpose. Heaven had an idea, and if it worked, everyone would be better off. She had on her skintight jeans, with only her sports bra. Reese loved it when she wore it, and Heaven was about to play off his ego. She would be doing something dangerous, and Rome knew nothing about it. It would be no way that he would allow her to see him after everything that he did to her.

She had lost her job because of him stalking her, and Heaven didn't care about that anymore. She didn't want to work for a company that had those views of people of her color. Heaven had more morals then that, she had an education, and was smart. She could quickly bounce back and get a better job. She was by herself, and the nerves started to kick in, Heaven hadn't seen Reese since the day at her job. The block was crowded, and she knew that he was out there; Reese didn't have anywhere else to be. She would argue with him about being on a block so much that cared nothing about him. Heaven could never get through to him; he was always fighting a war for a block that he didn't even own. She didn't understand that logic, and Heaven was out of her element. She didn't even tell Rome about her plan. Heaven figured that she could use his love for her to get him to end this bullshit with Rome. It was pointless, and nobody else needed to get hurt. Heaven pulled the car over, and they all stared at her, they knew who she was, and she could see Reese sitting on the hood of his car.

He looked at her, and he chuckled. Reese was feeling himself, and always said that she would come back running to him. It was no other reason in his mind why she would be here. Reese started to smile and could see the sports bra she was wearing through the window. He stood up and rubbed his hands together. Reese thought that having money is what got his woman back, and he knew that Rome couldn't handle a woman like Heaven. He was the only man that could give him what she needed. Reese waited patiently for her to step in the car. Heaven saw him watching, and she knew how he thought. It made her skin crawl because she knew what he was thinking. Heaven's heart was beating fast, and she didn't know why, she didn't know what Reese would do. She didn't realize how crazy and unstable he was until now. Sometimes it takes a person to step back to see what was right in front of them the entire time. She could mess this up, or Reese would lose his mind. She was trying to save Rome from killing Reese; Heaven could see it in his eyes. He was going to do it soon, and it would be more than a robbery, but murder.

She stepped out of the car, and her hips switched from side to side, and she caught the attention of every man that was outside. Reese bit his bottom lip, and he missed feeling her warm insides. Reese wanted to make love to her right now, and he had to get her back. But he had the ego thing going, and couldn't seem soft around his friends. She held her purse tight as she stood in front of him.

" Fuck you doing here, Heaven? You made it clear that you ain't fucking with me," Rome said.

" Can we talk inside your car; I don't want all these niggaz in our business?" Heaven asked.

Reese tried to act like he was thinking about what she asked him. He already had his mind made up about what he would do; Reese opened the door and stepped inside and waited for her to get in. " Whatever!"

Heaven was smiling inside, and her heart was pumping beyond hard. Nobody knew what she was about to do but Fatboy. He never got rid of the gun that was used to kill two of Gotti's goons, and she now had it back in her purse. She was going to place it underneath his seat, and then he would be gone was once the cops found it.

" So, what's the deal? How long are we going to go back and forth? You got me fired from my job, and you got arrested. I don't want us to be enemies, Reese. I will always love you," Heaven said, lying through her teeth.

" I love you too, forever. Come back to me, Heaven. We belong together, and you know I'm right," Reese said, thoughtfully.

Heaven sat her purse on the floor, and she was waiting on Fatboy's signal. He told her she would know when to leave the gun underneath his seat, and not long after that, it was a loud commotion outside. " Are they shooting! Oh, naw! I'm leaving!"

" Wait! Wait! Let me see what's going on?" Reese stepped out of the car.

Heaven took the gun out her purse that was wrapped in a white towel and placed it underneath the seat and placed the towel back in her bag. She almost got caught as the door opened back up, and he stepped back inside.

" I don't know what that was, but you are safe with me. Let's work on us, bae. I need you, fuck Rome! Meet for dinner, and we can talk about it more, I'll take us to our spot," Rome was smiling. He had no idea that his fate had been sealed.

" I'll call you later tonight. Pick the phone up; I'm leaving. You got too much shit going on right now, and I'm not getting shot for nobody," Heaven got back out the car and smiled all the way back to her car. It was nothing she wouldn't do for Rome, and it was nothing he wouldn't do for her, and it's been that way since they were eight years old. They were more than friends, and it was a love for the ages.

#

" Yo, you shouldn't even be here, Stinky! What kind man am I if I put you in danger like this??" Rome said, sitting in front of Reese's spot. He didn't think that it was a good idea, but Heaven knew everything about Reese. She knew all about the spots, and where he kept all the money. Reese had his money scattered throughout the city. He didn't keep all his eggs in one basket, but lucky for Rome, Heaven knew where all the eggs were hidden. He couldn't do this without her, and he never thought that they would be on a robbery spree together. Rome didn't have friends as liked as he was; he only had Heaven. She was the only real friend that he had, and without her, he would be all alone. He was grateful to have her by his side, and he was afraid to lose her. For the first time in his life, he thought about the possibility of losing her friendship. Being in a relationship was cool, but he valued being her friend more. He couldn't picture a world without Heaven.

She looked at him with a stern look on her face, and Rome never saw her so serious. It was so much hate built up for Reese after learning the truth. She was all on board, and was going to hold him down. She was ready for whatever came with them being together. Heaven knew that Rome was right, and they could live out their childhood dreams. What was stopping them from being everything they said they would be. She believed in them, and needed Rome to believe again too. They were only eight, but who's to say that they were only dreams. She would chase them forever with Rome by her side. It was the moment that Rome remembered everything about him that made her a believer. Rome didn't forget one detail, and she never thought he was listening, but he was all this time. Rome accepted her at her worse, and always placed her on a pedestal. He treated her like she was beyond special, she watched him move from girl to girl, and didn't think he was capable of love. But Heaven was wrong; he was waiting for his Stinky all this time.

" You are the best man; I have ever been around. That's who you are, Rome. This will be easy, and with him going to jail, it's like taking candy from a baby. Reese doesn't trust anyone, bae! Nobody it's in there, go in and take the shit, and we'll go to the next spot," Heaven explained. Rome couldn't help but smile, he never saw this side of her before, and he was liking it. Rome knew that he was probably moving too fast by having thoughts of marrying, Heaven. But he didn't care and already had in his mind what ring he would buy her. When Heaven talked, Rome listened. He knew how she wanted her wedding to be and everything. Rome's goal was to give her everything she had ever wanted, and he wouldn't stop until it was complete. Rome checked the clip in his gun and tucked it at his waist. He didn't want to get out of the car, and leave her by herself. Rome couldn't sit in front of Reese's spot forever, and he would have to make his mind up and soon. He grabbed her hand and took a deep breath, he kissed it and chuckled. He would make her his wife when this was over with, and was all the motivation he needed.

Heaven could see the reservations he was having, and loved that he cared about her so much. But Heaven was a boss chick, and was far from weak; she could handle herself. She would no longer let her fears stop her from being great. She already wasted so many years from being with him because of fear; she wasn't about to be like that anymore.

" Hey, you got this, bae! I gave you all the codes, go and get that shit and I'll watch out," Heaven said.

" How'd I get so lucky with you?" Rome asked.

" I don't know, now hurry up," Heaven said, pushing him out the car.

Rome stepped out the car and placed his mask over his face, he walked around to the back door, and was ready to enter the code to go inside, and it was a guy guarding the entrance. Rome leaned his back against the wall, and took a deep breath. He was almost spotted, but quickly stepped back before he could be seen. He waited until the guy turned his back to smoke a cigarette, and he hit him on the back of the head with the butt of the gun, knocking him out cold.

" Motherfucka!" Rome yelled. He wasn't taking any chances, and hit him again to make sure that he wasn't getting up. He entered the code that she gave him, and Heaven was right. The light turned green, and the steel door opened. Rome knew precisely where to go, he walked inside and cautiously wandered around. He went to where the safe was at, and cracked it opened. The green money was shining bright like the sun, and he started to stuff his bag quickly. But he heard the sound of a gun clicking at the back of his head.

" You pick the wrong spot to rob, nigga!" The second guard said.

Rome through his hands up in the air and cursed underneath his breath. " Fuck!" He knew that it was over, and he waited for him to pulled the trigger. He closes his eyes, and the sound of a gun going off echoed loudly. It sounded like a bomb was being dropped, and Rome opened his eyes slowly and searched his body for a hole. He was surprised to be alive, and the large guard body smacked the floor, making a loud thud.

Heaven stood there, holding a gun with smoke coming from the barrel. Her hand was shaking, and she couldn't move.

" I told your ass to stay in the car, Stinky!" Rome took the gun.

" I saw him coming in, and I had to do something, Rome! Is he dead?" Heaven asked.

" Dead then a motherfucka!" Rome finished stuffing his bag with money until it was empty. Let's go! Damn, I love you! Us forever!"

" Us forever," Heaven responded. They spent the rest of the night hitting every spot that Reese had, and when they got back home, it was over a half of million dollars in the bed. Rome and Heaven would never look back after this day, but the trouble was far from over. She picked up her phone and made a call to the police, and made an anonymous tip about the gun that was in Reese's car that was used to kill Gotti's goons.

#

Reese held his hand over his head in total shock. He was smoking blunts back to back and didn't believe that every one of his spots was hit last night. He thought he was smart by not putting all his money in one place. Reese only had the money he had in drugs that were on the street, and everything else was gone. Only one person knew about all his spots and knew all his codes. Something in his heart told him to change his passwords, but a part of him thought that he would get back with Heaven. He always thought she would come running back to him, but he was wrong. He never thought that they wouldn't get back together, but want Reese fell to realize that it was never going to work. Heaven and Reese would never have the connections of soulmates, and that's what she had with Rome. He thought that his money would always keep her around, and that was the biggest mistake he could have made. Reese thought he was untouchable, and he could cheat, and come in all times of the night. He never stood a chance the moment that Rome was released from jail; he was doomed when their eyes locked again. Heaven always knew that he was cheating on her, and she put up with it. Rome strangely showed her that she was worth way more the Reese.

Nobody knew shit, and it had Reese ready to kill, he wanted his money back, and he wanted his shit back now. Reese kept his money out the hood, but this last spot he was in now was dead in the middle of the block. It was crowded because of how hot it was outside, it was a typical summer day, and the kids played, the corn man walked down the street selling cups of fruit. Reese knew that somebody saw something, and he wanted answers. He didn't care what he had to do to get his shit back. He would put the pressure of the streets, but deep down, Reese knew who had his money. He was trying not to believe that Heaven would betray him like this, as if leaving him for Rome wasn't enough. Reese smacked his workers around, and he wanted to know how every spot got hit without then killing a motherfucka. He was stripped of his money, and now his freedom was next. Reese was about to lose everything, and it was all because of his jealousy of another man.

The police sirens went off loudly, and they invaded the block with more the ten squad cars. Reese took a deep breath, he figured that something happened outside, and never imagine that they were here for him. He wanted to be nosey like the next person, and he stepped on the porch. He looked at them all get out the car and point their guns at him. Reese looked around like they were crazy. They had a warrant to search his vehicle, and the lead detective approached him and showed him the paperwork. Reese read over it and shrugged his shoulders. He didn't have shit to hide, and he never kept shit in his car, all they would find was maybe some weed, so he thought. The officer searched his car, and it didn't take long for them to find the gun. He held it up in the air, and Reese shook his head. He was having one hell of a day; it was no way that it was his gun. He instantly thought that they were setting him up. He started to screamed at the officers as they placed him in cuffs.

" That's not my fuckin' gun! Yo, y'all planted that shit in my car!" Reese shouted. " I want to talk to a Captain! That's not mine!" Reese saw Rome and Heaven standing the crowd, and it clicked in his head. It was all Heaven's doing, and she put that gun in his car that day.

" Reese, you are under arrest for the murders of James Wright, and Londell Johnson," The officer started to read Reese his rights.

" Heaven, you are going to pay for this bitch! This ain't over! I'm innocent! I'm coming for you! That dirty bitch set me up!" Reese screamed at the top of his lungs as they placed him in the back of the squad car.

Heaven and Rome both placed their sunglasses on and laughed. They disappeared in the crowd, and he held onto her hand. " I love you, Stinky! One down, and one more to go."

CHAPTER THIRTEEN

Fatboy walked inside his house, and to his surprise, Jazzy was inside the kitchen with a cut off shirt that exposed her belly. She only had on a pink thong that was hugged inside her ass, he stopped in his tracks and bit his bottom lip. They were getting closer and closer as time passed, Fatboy wasn't going to say anything, but Jazzy was opening up to him in ways that he didn't think was possible. She was comfortable around him, and they did everything together now. You couldn't see him without seeing her sitting on the passenger side of his Range Rover. Jazzy could deny how she was feeling, and it was what she was trying to avoid. She would let her guard down, and that's when everything would change, but she had a feeling things would be different this time. Fatboy gave her a key to his house, and she never used it until now. She didn't want to be alone tonight and came over to fix him dinner. Things weren't supposed to go this way, and Jazzy was glad that it did. She smiled when she heard the keys inside the door, and her eyes lit up like a kid on Christmas Day.

She loved to be around him, and Jazzy may have
played a hard role, but she had a soft for him. Fatboy
smelled the food, and it made his stomach growl. In
his hand was a bag with a neckless inside that he
bought for her. He couldn't help but spoil her every
chance he got, Fatboy wanted to show her how much
he loved her. He walked up behind her and kissed the
side of her face. Fatboy could get used to seeing her
when he came home, and he lifted the pot top off to
see what she was cooking. Jazzy tapped his hand, and
he chuckled. They both stared into each other's eyes,
and the sparks began to fly. They had sex so many
times before, but it was always just that, only sex. It
was no emotions attach to it, and Fatboy wanted to
change that. He wanted to make love to her, and
Jazzy wanted that with him. She turned around and
wrapped her arms across his neck. She kissed him and
tasted the peppermint gum he was chewing on his
tongue. Fatboy's dick grew inside his pants, and he
palms her ass.

" No, Fatboy. I look a hot mess, I don't have my
makeup on or my eyelashes," Jazzy giggled. None of
that mattered to Fatboy, and she was sexy to him
without any of that. He smiled and didn't say
anything. He took the neckless out of the bag, and he
opened the box. Jazzy eyes got big, and she covered
her mouth with her hands. She couldn't help but let a
tear drop from her eyes. This was the thing that she
missed with being in a relationship. Jazzy loved that
he didn't change her, Fatboy accepted her flaws and

all. She kissed him passionately, and he started to rub his hands all across her body, and Jazzy let off a seductive moan. He lifted her from off her feet and sat her down on the kitchen table. He removed her thong and grabbed a strawberry from the fridge, and he dangled it in front of Jazzy's lips. They both shared a seductive kiss, and they ate the strawberry together. He slowly rubbed his hand across her breast, and her hard nibbles enjoyed his sweet touch.

" Fatboy, I don't want to mess this up, you doing something to me," Jazzy whispered seductively.

" I won't fuck this up, and I promise," he mumbled with her breast inside his mouth. She rubbed her hands through his curly hair, and he moved lower and lower until her pussy was on his face. He sucked her clit, and she leaned her head back. He gave her slow licks, and she placed her hands on his head. Fatboy teased her and took the whipped cream and placed if all over her body. Jazzy became his human canvas as he explored every inch of her. It was all over his face, and her stomach, and Jazzy jumped down from the counter and prompted her leg up, and he slid his dick inside her. He grabbed the back of her hair, and he fucked her slow. It was nothing like the chubby dick strokes he was giving her, so he thought.

" Fatboy," Jazzy yelled out as pure pleasure took control over her body. He increased his speed, and she through her ass back in sync with each stroke he gave her. Jazzy ass started to jiggle like it was filled with water. Her love juice was on the tip of his dick, and it was nothing more important than the two of them at the moment. Jazzy was in love, and it had always been there for him, but now she was finally able to let it out.

" I'll never do you wrong, and I love you, Jazzy," Fatboy said.

" I love you, too," Jazzy said for the first time. Their bodies started to sweat as they switch positions all night. They made their way into the bedroom, and they made love in the purest form. It was different than either of them had ever experienced. It was nothing like it, and Jazzy and Fatboy continued to make love until the sun came up. They were officially together, and he would forever ride for his Jazzy.

#

Heaven couldn't get the smile from off her face, thinking about what Rome and her had pulled off. They had a ton of money, and Reese was out of her life for good. She focused on her life with Rome now. She sat next to Jazzy as they both sat in the courtroom. The had to see the judge for the assault case they had fuckin' around with Kat. She couldn't help but notice the smile on Jazzy face. It was nothing to be smiling about, but yet they both were. If found guilty, they both could face up to a year in prison. Heaven had never been arrested before, but Jazzy, on the other hand, was no stranger to the judicial system. She had been in and out of jail since she was a kid for beating bitches up, it was kind of her thing. She now wished that she had a better upbringing. Jazzy needed to learn how to control her temper; she needed anger management, and that was clear. Heaven wanted to tell her about the money they had from hitting Reese's spots, but this wasn't the time nor place to do that. It was killing her not being able to tell Jazzy, and she couldn't wait until this bullshit was over.

Jazzy looked at Kat sitting on the other side of the courtroom, and wanted to walk over and bust her damn head open. Fatboy was able to get them the best lawyer in the state, and Jazzy wasn't worried, but that was about to change. Her background was about to come back up to haunt her. She didn't know how she was even up, and Jazzy hadn't been to sleep. She was in love for the first time in years, but Jazzy didn't want to get her hopes up too high: she was so afraid of getting her heart broke; it was preventing her from enjoying the love that Fatboy was giving her. He sat in the back row, and he wasn't not going to show up to support her. They kept giving each other the eye the entire time, and Heaven thought that it was weird. She missed Rome, and wished that he could have been there. He had to meet with his P.O. and she needed him right now. She was nervous, and couldn't stop tapping her leg. Heaven didn't want to go to jail, and courtrooms always made her feel a particular type of way.

That last time she was here was when the judge gave Rome his time, and she could still remember the feeling she had when they took him into the back. She didn't want to go through that. Kat sat over there, and her mind was on Bugs, and she didn't hear from Rome yet. She didn't know if they told him, but if she didn't live up to her end of the bargain, then she was dead. Kat didn't even want to show up for this shit; it made her look like a snitch. But she didn't need more trouble at her doorstep, so she showed up. Kat didn't even want to press charges and tried to tell them that she didn't want to move forward with the case, but it was too late for that now. Jazzy smacked her lips; she couldn't stand Kat. Fatboy could see the anger in Jazzy and leaned over, whispering in her ear. She smiled and sat back in her seat, Jazzy was in the beginning stages of love, and the sound of his voice made her pussy wet. Heaven looked at her phone to check the time, and saw that she was late. She already didn't want to be there, and wanted to get this shit over and done with as soon as possible.

After another ten minutes of waiting their Jewish lawyer cane walking in with a wrinkled suit on and his hair slicked back, Heaven frowned her face up. He didn't look like the best lawyer in the state, but he was, according to Fatboy. His appearance was off, but he always got the job done. He signaled for Jazzy and Heaven to follow him to the hallway.

" Okay, so here's what's going to happen, I have bad news and good news, so I'll rip the bandage off now. Jazzy, the judge is looking to give you jail time. The state asked for six months in the county jail because of her background. You have four other assault cases, and they are looking to make an example out of you. Heaven, on the other hand, this is your first case, so they are offering community service," the lawyer explained.

" Six months? I barely touched that damn girl! I'm about to fuck this bitch up, and then they could take my ass to jail. Fuck that! Let's go to trial!" Jazzy had smoke coming from her nose, she was on fire, and was ready to pop off. Her temper had finally gotten her in trouble, and it was nothing he could do.

" I wouldn't recommend going to trial; if we lose, the state can give you three years. It several witnesses that saw the both of y'all. We take the deal, and you'll be out in three months with good behavior. It's the best deal we can get, I can have the judge give you a three-week stay to get your affairs in order," the lawyer said skimming through his notes.

" Fuck it! I'll do the time! I'm a bad bitch! I'll do that time like a G! Let's do it, and I'm throwing a huge going away party! That shit going to be lit!" Jazzy walked back into the courtroom, leaving them standing there looking stupid.

He pointed his finger at Jazzy as she walked off. " She's not going to fight her again, is she?"

" Yeah, we better get inside there!" Heaven giggled.

#

Rome stared at all the money on the bed, and was in awe. He never saw so much at one time before, and even with the money, he only cared about Heaven. He lied to her and said that he couldn't make her court date, but he didn't want to waste any time. Rome wanted to get her a ring why he had the money. He didn't know what would happen, and he went out and got her the ring she always dreamed of when they were kids. He held the wedding ring up inside the box, and his heart was beating fast. He was about to ask his best friend to marry him, and he wasn't sure if she would say yes. Rome had all kinds of doubts in his mind; he wanted to be the perfect husband to Heaven, and didn't want to disappoint her. He was going back and forth with himself on should he ask her now, no time was the right time Rome thought. He always told her when they were kids that he would ask her, but it was kids talking about things they would do when they got older. He has been secretly waited on this day to come forever, he had how he felt for so long, but that was done now.

The mood was set, and Rome had the house exactly how Heaven said she wanted her proposal to be, it was the middle of the day, so he had all the blinds closed. It was candles lit on the floor, leading to a bunch of rose petals shaped like a heart. He didn't know what he would say, and figured that he would speak from the heart. They only person who knew that he was about to do was Jazzy. It was hard to keep them having all Reese's money from Jazzy because she asked him so many questions. He was able to pull it off, and now he was about to take a leap of faith and prayed that it would work out. Rome couldn't see himself being with anyone else; she was the only woman that knew him, and understood him. She accepted him with his flaws and all, how could he not want to spend the rest of his life with Heaven. He was practicing all morning how he would get on one knee, but it was no perfect way. Rome knew that she would be walking in any second, and it would be game time.

He kept looking out the window, hoping to see her car pull up, he checked his phone for a text message and nothing. Rome wanted to get this shit over with, so he could calm his ass down. His biggest fear was her saying no to him, and that would crush his soul. Rome would be hurt, but it wouldn't stop him from being her friend. That was a bond that was for life, and he wasn't going to allow anything to stop that. They had developed something unknown to mankind, and that was more important to him then her saying yes. He knew that Heaven was here now because he could hear the car pulling up. He checked the scenes and made sure everything was right. He looked around and told himself that it was game time. The hairs on his arms began to stand up, and the butterfly feeling was in the pit of his stomach. The door opened, and he stood in the center of white rose petals shaped like a heart.

Heaven stopped in her tracks, and it clicked in her mind. She immediately knew what this was, and she started to cry. Jazzy had the biggest smile on her face, and she was so happy for her friend. Heaven couldn't believe that he remembered; it was like he didn't forget any conversation they had as kids. She loved him even more at that moment. It was precisely how she wanted it to be, and Heaven was scared to walk further into the house. She turned to Jazzy and playfully hit her across the arm.

" You knew about this, didn't you, bitch?" Heaven asked.

" He made me promise not to say anything," Jazzy smiled.

Rome didn't wait or hesitate; he held out his hand and waited for Heaven to come towards him. She held her hand over her mouth, and the tears of joy came down her cheek. She didn't know what to say, but she did know that she wasn't going to say no.

" Yes! Yes! Yes!" Heaven said prematurely. He didn't have to ask her; she was down for him always.

" I didn't ask you anything," Rome chuckled. He got down on one knee and spoke from the heart. " We would always say that it is us forever, and I would like to make that official. You make me a better man, and couldn't picture life without you, Heaven. You are my muse, and the beacon to my existence. I promise always to love you and never to change up on you. So, with that being said, will you marry me, Stinky?"

" Yes! Hell, yes!" Heaven said. She watched as he put the ring on her finger, and she couldn't believe it. Jazzy recorded everything on her phone, and she was inspired. She found faith in love again, watching Rome and Heaven.

Rome stood up from the floor, and they kissed passionately. She wrapped her arms tightly around him. They had been together every day since they were eight years old, and they were now making it official. They would spend the rest eternity with each other, and it was a moment that would go down in history. It was the beginning of a perfect union between two beautiful people.

" I'm so happy for y'all! Let's get drunk! My bitch is getting married, and I'm going to jail! I think that deserves for us to get wasted. I love y'all!" Jazzy said. She was right, and Heaven looked at her husband and got lost in his eyes.

CHAPTER FOURTEEN

Rome had a different demeanor about him now, and that's what money did to people. He wasn't going to let it changed him; Rome wasn't going to be that person. He wasn't through yet, and he still had to hit Gotti. Rome walked out of the help center and tossed his sunglasses on his face. His mother was still fighting an ongoing battle with her drug problem. He wasn't getting his hopes up, but the fact that his mother was trying was good enough for him. Lisa had a one day pass to go out and see her family. She didn't want to use her pass because Lisa knew that she would use, but this weekend she wanted to surprise her son. He was a man now, and to see him through sober eyes was the best feeling in the world to her. She was doing it for him, and more importantly, Lisa wanted to show G-Mama that she was clean. Things were looking good for Rome, and he knew this day would come one day. He walked carefree through the blocks with his gun on his hip. He didn't want to have to use it, but he would. Reese was gone, and he didn't know who was coming after him.

He was thinking about having children as he walked to his car; Rome was having so many thoughts going on in his mind. He thought he would be a good dad; Rome was still trying to find his purpose. He thought the money would take that feeling away from him, but it didn't. He was still struggling with what he wanted to do with his life. That money wasn't going to last forever, and then what was he going to do. Rome had a lot of things to think about, but it was one thing he knew for certain, and that was he didn't want to be a dopeboy. That wasn't his time of thing, and he wanted more out his life. Rome felt like walking and didn't take his car. He saw kids who were called the " Bucket Boys" doing their thing. He gave them a hundred dollar bill and kept walking. That was how it was in the hood; everyone had a hustle. Rome was searching for his, and he definitely couldn't be a professional robber. He needed something legit that he was good at, and he could make a lot of money. Rome did not doubt that he would find his way, and with Heaven with him, how could he fail.

" You are going to keep me in the friend zone forever," the small boy said to a girl standing on her porch. Rome couldn't help but laugh, and it made his mind go back to when Heaven and him would have those same conversations. He used to think that he was so cool back then, but he was far from that. Rome admires young love, and to him, it was the purest form of love there was, it always did something to him. Rome loved to walk through the blocks; he didn't always need to drive. He needed time to think, and he couldn't stop thinking about his mother. He was so proud of her; it was a massive deal for her to get clean. She was barely three weeks clean, but it was a start. When he saw that she had a pass, it was going to drive him crazy. Lisa should have told him, but she wanted it to be a surprise, and that was the biggest mistake that she could have ever made. People in the world didn't want to see Rome do good; he walked without a doubt that his mother was about to be a target as she walked out of the help center.

Lisa smelled the fresh air as it smacked her in the face; she smiled. The thought of swing G-Mama seeing her doing good was the best thing for her. She never saw Gotti following her, and Lisa stopped at the bus stop. She only had a twenty-four-hour pass, and she had to be right back, or they would kick her out of the program. It was working for her and was applying the steps to her everyday life, and she didn't have the desire to use.

Gotti pulled up in a black sedan and let the window down. " Lisa, is that you? Damn, you look good!"

" Hey, Gotti! Did you see Rome he just left; I've been three weeks clean? I'm going to see G-Mama," Lisa was blind to what was going on with Gotti and her son. The last thing she remembered was them being cool, so Lisa didn't take him as a threat.

" I'm happy for you! Where are you going? You need a ride, and I can take you," Gotti said with a

devilish grin on his face. He would hurt Rome, where
it hurts him the most, and that was his mother.

" Uh, yeah, sure," Lisa walked around and
stepped in the car. She smiled, and something was
telling her to get out, but she decided against it. She
ignored her inner thoughts and rode in silence, she
didn't know what was going on, but something wasn't
right. " Where we going? This not the way to G-
Mama's house."

" I have to make a quick stop, and it's not going
to take long. You got something special planned for
today?" Gotti said.

" Nothing much, I just want some family time,"
Lisa responded.

Gotti pulled the car off and got out purposely,
dropping two bags of heroin on the seat. Lisa stared
at the bags of dope, and knew that she should have
gotten out the car and left. But she wasn't strong
enough yet, and was early in her recovery. She
snatched the two bags of dope and got out of the car.

#

" So, you all in love and shit now. Why you ain't
tell me that you and Fatboy were together now. I've
been telling you for months to give him a chance,"
Heaven said with smoked filled lungs. She was so
happy for her friend, and Heaven had a pair of
Chanel shades on even though she knew that was a
no-no, her entire swag had changed in a matter of
days. Jazzy and Heaven sat on the porch and enjoyed

the summer day. They were the two baddest chicks in the hood, and everyone knew it. They both were dropped down in designer clothes, and watched the girls jump rope, and the boys play basketball in the middle of the street. Heaven couldn't help but keep looking at her wedding ring. If you had told her months ago that she would be marrying her best friend, she would have told you that you were crazy. But it was happening, and not only that, but Jazzy was in love with her friend too. It was like some love out of a Disney movie; Heaven wasn't going to complain. She was going to sit back and enjoy the moment.

" The same reason you ain't tell me about you and Rome robbing Reese blind," Jazzy giggled. Heaven looked around like the FEDS was listening. She playfully hit her friend, and puffed her blunt. She hated that Rome was still working at the hotdog stand, and Heaven laughed when she thought about it. Rome would threaten to quit almost every day; by he ended up right back there. She was fearful for his life, he worked in Gotti's hood, and at any second they could get to him. She knew that he could take care of himself, but that didn't stop her from worrying. Heaven and Jazzy laughed and joked as they got high; they were trying to decide what they were going to wear to Fatboy's party. Every year he would throw one of the biggest parties to cap the summer off, and everyone was going to be there. If you were somebody you would be there, and all the rappers would show up, that's how big it was going to be. Jazzy stood up and stretched out her body; she hadn't jumped rope in years. The weed had her still thinking could she still do it. She walked over with Heaven.

" Can I get a turn? I think I still got it, Heaven turn for me," Jazzy said. She was high and hoped that she didn't fall flat on her damn face. Heaven grabbed the robe, and Jazzy waited until the right moment, and she jumped inside. It was like riding a bike as it all clicked back in her mind. She did her thing, and she skipped all around the rope with style, and it went on for a long time until finally, her feet got tangled in the rope. She was out of breath, and Heaven hugged her, and they both started to laugh. It was days like this that Heaven was going to miss; she knew that they couldn't stay in the hood forever. It was so much good that happened here, and the news didn't report that. It wasn't all about the shootings and drugs, but moments like this are what made the hood special. It was an indescribable feeling, and you had to be from here to understand that Jazzy, and Heaven was feeling right now. It was a joy you could only find in the ghetto, and that's what Heaven loved so much about it.

Jazzy shook her head when she saw Twin walking up the street, and she knew that he was about to hit her for some money. She couldn't tell him no, before the drugs Twin was a major player in the city, and use to be in love with Jazzy's mother. He helped raise her, and how could she not look out for him whenever he asked.

" Where's Rome? I have some bad news; he needs to get his ass down here now!" Twin shouted.

" Why? What's going on, Twin?" Heaven asked. She was now worried and hoped that it wasn't anything that bad.

Twin almost didn't want to say anything, but the entire hood knew about Lisa's recovery and the new how well she was doing. He didn't want to see her like this, but Twin found her high as a kite in the spot. She almost looked like she was one high away from overdosing; she had some stuff that was stronger than what was being sold on the streets. Gotti had given her something that could possibly kill her, and he wanted to make sure she fell entirely off her sobriety.

" I found his mother, and she's not doing good. She's using again, and I don't know where she got this shit from, but it's not good. That's the shit that kills people, and she's doing bad. I thought he would want to go and get her. If she gets high again off that shit, she will die," Twin explained. He didn't even want money for his information; he felt that bad for Lisa.

Heaven covered her mouth with her hand, and she didn't know what to say. She didn't want to upset Rome, but she knew that she had to tell him. It was going to crush him, and she was doing so good, she didn't know how this happened. " Oh, my god. Where is she, Twin?"

" She's down at the spot; you need to go get her now!" Twin shouted.

Jazzy shook her head, and the joy was snatched from that quick. Heaven held her head low, and she picked up her phone to dial Rome's number. They would have to go down there and help her. They had no idea that this was all Gotti's doing, and that he wasn't going to go away anytime soon. Heaven knew that Rome wasn't ready to see his mother like that.

#

Rome pulled up in his car, and almost jumped out before he could put the car in park. He had just left his mother, and she was fine, so he couldn't understand how this happened. She was doing so well, and how did it happen so fast. Something wasn't adding up to Rome, he walked up, and Heaven stood in front of an abandoned house that was boarded up. She didn't go inside yet, but Twin made it clear that she was inside. She almost didn't want to tell him because she knew this was going to send him down a dark path. He was so happy now, and they were going to get married. She couldn't understand why she kept hurting him, and it had been this way for years. She realized that it was his mother, but Lisa wasn't ready to get clean, and Rome couldn't force her to be a better person. He would have let go and let God do the rest. But it wasn't the case this time, Lisa wanted to get clean, and Gotti changed that. He was jealous of Rome, and always had been. That on top of him secretly wanting to be with him on the downlow, Gotti was afraid to live his truth, he figured that he couldn't be a gay goon.

Heaven hugged Rome tightly. He looked around and instantly felt like something was off, why was his mother and in Gotti's hood. She was never over here, and now she was, that didn't sit right with him. Rome shrugged it off to his mother, being an addict, and going wherever the drug took her. A part of him wanted to wash his hands with the situation and wanted to give up on her, and leave her ass in there. But Rome wanted to know why she would give up everything again chasing the first high. Rome walked inside the building, and the strong smell made him cover his nose. It stunk of urine and all types of other things. He held his shirt up over his nostrils. Neighborhood fiends were scattered across the house, and it was like the Walking Dead. People stumbled as they walked like zombies, and Rome never saw it up close like this before. It was a sight to behold, and he searched around for his mother, and it took him a while to find her. She was laid up against a wall on the floor with a belt still wrapped around her arm.

Lisa looked up with a smile after seeing his face, and that quickly turned into tears once she realized that she was high. Rome never saw her cry like that before, not even when his father was killed. She wanted to get clean, but she wasn't ready for a pass, and let alone to be left alone with dope. She couldn't resist the temptation, and it was too much for her.

Jazzy shook her head; she always loved the glitz and glamor side of the dopeboy's. But this was the other side, and it was the part that everyone brushed to the side. It was the outcome of the drugs that were being pumped into the black community. He tried to pick her up to carry her out, but Lisa was beyond high. It was like Lisa's legs weren't working, and they gave out on her. She fell to the floor and let out a crazy laugh. She started to rock back and forth with a massive smile on her face. Rome looked at Heaven, and shook his head in disappointment. He wanted to be done with his mother, but he wasn't that person. He was pissed off and decided never to sell drugs again. He couldn't do his people like that anymore.

Lisa dropped her syringe, and Rome crushed it with his boot. He wanted to know how she was able to get out, and where did she get money to buy drugs that fast. He bent down, and she rubbed the side of his face. He didn't know the words to say; all he knew was he had to get her back to the help center. It was a habit that she was going to need help with; he didn't care what anyone said; he couldn't turn his back on her.

" You were doing so good, Ma. What happened? Why did you leave the help center?" Rome asked. He helped her back up from the ground.

Lisa reached into her pocket and showed him her pass for twenty-four hours. " I was going to surprise, G-Mama, and show her how good I was doing. That she could call me her daughter again, I want my mother back, Rome. You can understand that, right?" Lisa said.

" Yeah, I get it. I have to take you back, Ma. It's the only way that you can get clean. What are you doing on Gotti's block?"

" I saw Gotti! He gave me a ride, and when he got out of the car, two bags of dope fell out of his pocket. So, I took it and left. I'm so glad that you have a good friend like him, Rome," Lisa mumbled.

Heaven looked at Rome and then Jazzy. They all had that look on their faces, and they knew what happened now. Rome didn't think that Gotti would stoop this low, and he wanted blood. All this was for what? Rome was trying to figure that part out, and he never did anything to him. Rome was cool with everyone in the hood, but that was the streets for you. It would be your best friend that would set you up for a couple of dollars. It was the world that we lived in, and it wasn't getting any better.

" Don't worry about it, Ma. We are going to get you clean; I promise!"

CHAPTER FIFTEEN

Fatboy stood on the block and passed out dollar bills as the kids swarmed him. It was everyday shit for him to pass out money women the ice cream truck came around. Fatboy was putting the finishing touches on his massive annual summer party. He wasn't looking forward to it again this year, and it would be the last day that Jazzy would be free. She had to turn herself in the next day to do six months in the county jail. He had just gotten used to waking up every morning with her by his side, and now she had to leave him. Fatboy wasn't feeling that shit at all, it wasn't a lot of time, so he figured that it would fly by, but that didn't make him feel any better. Seeing Rome ask Heaven to marry him made her want to have that one day; he wasn't a fool and knew that him and Jazzy were ready for that now. But it was always a possibility for the future. He could see himself being her husband, and smiled as he thought about it. Fatboy was well-loved, and he looked out for his block. He paid people's rent, car notes, and whatever else they asked him. He rarely told people no.

He was counting the seconds down until Jazzy pulled up, he was spending less and less time on the block, and it was because of Jazzy. He was loving being laid up with her, and it was even better than he used to imagine. Fatboy fixed the gun that was on his waist, so the kids didn't see it. He never left home without it, Fatboy had been shot already back in the day, and he wasn't going to be caught slippin' again. Especially with Gotti roaming the street. That was beef that went back years, they never got alone, and never will. Gotti didn't like Fatboy because he couldn't control him, and that's when the hating began. Fatboy was his own boss, and would never see himself taking orders from a nigga like Gotti. He passed out the last dollar and leaned up against the side of his car. Fatboy wished it was a way to get Jazzy out of the jail time she had to do. He wanted to leave the country with her, but now he would have to put that on hold because of some dumb shit. Fatboy's frowned his face up when he saw Kat approaching him.

" I should kill this, bitch," Fatboy said. Everyone knew how grimy Kat was, and she would do anything for a dollar. He tried to warn Rome about her as everyone else did in the beginning, and he didn't listen. Kat was moving on borrowed time, if she didn't bring Gotti, and Bugs something for her trying to steal from them. She wrote a check her ass couldn't get cash this time. She had completely ruined her relationship with Rome, and it was no way she could deliver him like she said. But she was hoping that they would take Fatboy instead, she had to try at least. She knew that Fatboy was known to fuck anything, and all she had to do was show interest, and he would be eating out the palm of her hand. But that was the old Fatboy, he wasn't that man anymore, and would never do anything to hurt Jazzy. Fatboy did those things because he didn't have Jazzy, and now that he did, he wouldn't even entertain another woman. She walked up and leaned up against the car next to him with a seductive look in her eyes.

Fatboy didn't know what she wanted, but all he knew was he wasn't about to fall for her bullshit. He had too much to lose now, and nothing was worth losing Jazzy, not even his money. Fatboy looked at her like she was crazy, and Kat had this sorry look in her eyes. She looked desperate, and that's exactly was she was right now. Kat had no choice, and she didn't have money to leave town; it was Fatboy life for hers, so she had to try and see if he would take the bait. If he didn't, she had no idea what she would do.

"The fuck do you want. My girl has to do six months because of your ass, you lucky I don't kill your ass. If it weren't for all these kids, I would. So, skip your ass right back up that street and leave me the fuck alone, whatever you are selling, I ain't buying, bitch," Fatboy said with authority in his tone.

Kat could see that this was going to be damn near impossible. She didn't know that him and Jazzy were a thing now. " Look, I didn't have shit to do with that, the state picked up the charges. I didn't even ask for them to lock her up, cut me some slack, I'm here to see you," Kat gave him the eye and rubbed her hand across the side of his face.

" Back your ass up, you better leave because Jazzy is about to pull up any second. I don't need her ass catching another case fuckin' with your bird ass!" Fatboy shouted, starting to walk off.

Kat had to do something and fast to let him know that she was serious. She ran and caught up with him, and at the same time, Jazzy pulled up. She kissed him and pushed her tongue down his mouth. He pushed her away, but it was too late, and all Jazzy saw was the kiss.

" What the fuck!" Jazzy yelled, jumping out the car. She locked eyes with Kat, and she took off running. Jazzy chased her down the street, but Kat was too fast. " I'm going to catch you, bitch!"

" Baby, I would never do that to you! I pushed her off me!" Fatboy pleaded his case.

Jazzy caught her breath and smacked him across his face. " You should have never been around that nasty, hoe! I should have just kept you the friend zone," Jazzy screamed.

"Fuck!" Fatboy yelled. It was the only words that came out his mouth, he let Jazzy leave, and hoped that she would cool off by the time he got home.

#

Jazzy couldn't believe what her eyes saw, and she figured that she had to be seeing shit. She started to cry, and this was the main reason she didn't want to be in a relationship with anyone. They could have stayed friends, and she wouldn't have this feeling in her stomach. She hated Kat with every fiber of her being, and now she had to go upstate. Jazzy played hard, but she was scared, and she wasn't going to let any bitches punk her, she was still afraid of the unknown. Jazzy had the ability to hold shit down whatever she went; it wouldn't take long before she would be running the jail. It would only make her go harder when she came home. She didn't know why she ended up at Fatboy's house. He had been caught kissing her enemy and started to think about who Fatboy was as a person. He was the man and could have any chick he wanted, so why would he give all that up for her. What made her so unique, and Jazzy was still trying to figure that out. Jazzy wanted to hurt something, but that would only get her further in trouble. She didn't have any weed, so her nerves were bad, and she started to put Fatboy's clothes in a tub, and she poured bleach on his clothes.

" I'm a bad, bitch! A hoe could never!" Jazzy said with the bottle of bleach in her hands. She was fucking everything up that Fatboy owns that she thought had value to him. She called and told Heaven what happened, and Jazzy couldn't believe that she took up for Fatboy. She wasn't trying to hear that shit even though she saw him pushed her away, and knew that Kat was a dirty person. She knew that it wasn't Fatboy fault, but Jazzy needed a reason to fight with him and end the relationship. It had nothing to do with the Kat and the kiss. But more with her scared to love Fatboy, and she did love him. Jazzy didn't tell him yet, and her burning his shit in the tub said it loud and clear. Fatboy gave her the keys to the kingdom, and she knew things that his closest comrades did know. She wasn't thinking clearly, and her reign of terror didn't stop there. She went back into the room and grabbed his Jordan's, and Balenciaga's shoes, and took the scissors.

" Baby, where you at? Fatboy said, walking through the door, he couldn't wait until she calmed down. He needed to talk to her now and let her see that he was serious about her, and that Kat shit wasn't real to him. That shit meant nothing to him, and however she wanted to handle it, he was down. Fatboy' was ready to lay his murder game down, and was willing to kill Kat, if that's what Jazzy wanted to do. Fatboy didn't kill women or children, but he would make an exception for Kat. She was causing too much trouble for him and Rome. He looked at Kat like a cancer, and she needed to be removed from the equation. Fatboy could smell the bleach because it was so strong. He made his way throughout the house, and Jazzy was sitting in the middle of the floor with his shoes cutting them into small pieces. His mouth dropped with he saw his thousand dollars

Balenciaga's ripped all up. Fatboy covered his head with his hands and chuckled.

Fatboy ran over and grabbed his shoes from her. Most of his shoes were gone, and it was no bringing them back. He couldn't even get mad, and he sat down on the sofa. He leaned his head back, and Jazzy got up and sat down next to him. Neither one of them said anything, and it was like it was nothing to be said. Jazzy looked at him, and the expression on his face said it all, and she knew then that that kiss meant nothing.

" My Jordan's, though! Why, Jazzy, you know I love my Jordan's, baby! Kat kissed me out the blue. You know, I don't want anything to do with that chick. You do know that, right?" Fatboy asked.

" Yeah, I know," Jazzy exhaled deeply.

" Then why you fuck all my shoes up, Jazzy!" Fatboy shouted. He picked up the pieces of his shoes, and his heart dropped. He couldn't do anything but laugh; he loved her crazy ass. He wanted her to trust him, but it was going to take time, Fatboy now understood that.

" I bleached your clothes too," Jazzy said, laughing. She thought it was funny. Jazzy leaned her head on his shoulder. " I love you, Fatboy."

" I love you, too. You are not getting off that easy! I got something for your ass," Fatboy got on his knees and snatched her pants off. He pulled her panties to the side and stuck his face deep in her pussy. He licked her clit, and she grabbed the top of his head. She let out a seductive moan, and spread her legs apart wide. He licked slow and then fast while tasting her sweet love juice.

" Fatboy! Wait?" Jazzy never in her life was about to climax that fast, and she arched her back. She pushed him away and ran out of the room. Fatboy smiled and stood up, wiping his face. He ran behind her into the room.

" Don't run now!" Fatboy chuckled.

#

Reese walked into the visiting room, wearing a bright orange jumpsuit with his hands shackled to his waist. His beard had grown, and he had a stern look on his face, Reese wasn't his usual self. He was stressed all the way out, and still had Heaven on his mind. She had turned on him, and stripped him of everything. Reese learned quickly that he didn't have any friends out in the streets. Nobody came to see him or even check on his moms. He could barely get people to answer his calls, and now he had a vendetta against everyone. Reese was charged with first-degree murder, and the had the gun that was used. He was about to fight a case that he didn't do, and he chalked it up as karma for all the bodies that he did do. Reese didn't know who was coming to see him, and at this point, he didn't care. All his money was gone, and the cash he had left on the street, the guys had stiffed him on. His crew split and left him for dead. The streets were a cold game, and now Reese knew that firsthand.

He wanted Rome dead, and he would do anything to get it done. If he had to spend his life in prison, then it was only right that Rome got his life taken too.

The large steel door made a buzzing sound, and the guard took he handcuffs from his wrist. Reese looked as Gotti was sitting on the other side of the thick glass, and worried what the fuck he was doing here. He didn't trust Gotti too, and if he was here, then that meant that he wanted something. Reese didn't know what he had to offer, and he took a deep breath as he sat down. He prayed that he could find a way to come from underneath this case. He would be right back because killing Rome would be number one on his list. Reese was a sucker for love, he still wanted to be with Heaven, and he knew that it was all Rome's doing. He was inside Heaven's head, and she needed to be reminded of how much he cared about her. Being inside a cell for twenty-three hours a day gave him time to think and realized that he played a significant part in losing Heaven. The money had him feeling untouchable, and now he understood that. But it was too late now, and he now had to suffer the consequences of his actions. He picked the phone up and placed it to his ear.

" Fuck you want?" Reese said into the phone. Gotti was being beat at every corner by Rome, and all he could do was attack his mother. He needed help, and that's why he was here with Reese now. Gotti had an idea that he couldn't help him, Reese was flat broke. It was nothing that Reese could offer; his crew went left on him. Gotti was sick of hiding from the world, and wanted to live his truth, but he loved the past more than coming out as a gay black man. He would rather live a lie than to lose his reign at the top. He thought what all this was about on the way over; he used to be friends with Rome. Gotti was mad that he couldn't have him, he was secretly in love with his friend, and because he couldn't have him, he stabbed him in the back. He started this shit, and regardless if they used to be friends, it had to be done. It hurts more when you have to kill a nigga that you love, and Gotti kept telling himself that.

Reese held the phone on the other end and waited for Gotti to speak. He didn't have time to bullshit around; his only focus was beating this murder. He knew that he couldn't, and that's what killed his spirit. So, whatever Gotti wanted, Reese didn't give a fuck so he could turn right back around and leave him the fuck alone. Reese shrugged his shoulders, and now had a look of irritation on his face.

" Yo, what the fuck you want?" Reese repeated.

" They entire hood know you ain't do that shit, how the fuck you let this happen. What are we going to do about that shit?" Gotti asked.

" We?" Reese chuckled. " You would know I didn't do that shit being that you were there, and your testimony could get me out," Reese said. He was moments from getting up and leaving.

Gotti was a stand-up nigga, you could call him all types of things, but a snitch isn't one of them. If he told, the streets would never respect him again. Power was a drug, and Gotti would never give up that high. " It's fucked up, Reese. But I ain't no rat! It has to be another way, and I would die before I snitch, you know that."

" I'm here for killing your people, and you were there, so save that street code bullshit! You better believe that they will tell on you, nigga! My entire crew left me, ain't no honor in the streets. So, again why are you here, Gotti!" Reese said, slamming the phone against the window. His anger was visible, and he didn't want to hear that shit.

" We can get Rome back together, and I just need your help," Gotti pleaded.

Reese scoffs and chuckled. " You need my help," he said mockingly.

Gotti shook his head because he knew that Reese wasn't in a good headspace, and he had every right to feel like the world was against him. But Gotti couldn't do it, he wasn't a rat, and if he had to do that to get his help, then he didn't need it.

" Don't ever come back here," Reese dropped the phone and stood up. " Guard! Take me back to my cell, we done here!"

CHAPTER SIXTEEN

G-Mama walked into the living room and tossed Rome's dream book down in front of him. She was tired of seeing him get hurt because of his mother, and it was time for him to let that shit go. She understood that it was his mother, and he had that special love for her, but he needed to move on with his life. G-Mama wanted to see him make it, and she saw the potential inside him. She tried to give him time to be a man, but she wasn't a fool. She knew that Rome was a street nigga, and if she could keep him for throwing his life away, then she would. She had to remind him of who he used to be. Rome had dreams of being the next Dapper Dan, and do his clothing line. He could still do that, if he fixed his way of thinking. This hood mentality was destroying black men, and G-Mama did want that for her grandson. She sat down next to him, and pushed the book in front of him, and he smiled. He knew what she was trying to do, and he was grateful. He needed a smile right now, and he could always count on her.

" Wow, you still have this book?" Rome opened it up, and he couldn't help but get lost in his thoughts.

It was all the things he wanted to do with his life, and Heaven was a part of everything. He couldn't believe that she had this after all this time, it was so much shit in there. Rome always wanted to start his own clothing line with Heaven called " West Avenue," and to see that again made him laugh. She was showing him this to remind him, but Rome still had doubt. He was just a kid when Heaven and him thought of this, and it was silly dreams that two kids for the hood had. Rome doubted that he could do that; he had so much on his mind right now, and starting a clothing line based on a childhood fantasy was the farthest thing from his mind. Rome was focused on one thing, and that was robbing Gotti. He would figure the rest of that shit out later.

He closed the book back and slid it back to G-Mama. She got up and slapped the back of his head, G-Mama tossed the book on his lap, and Rome laughed. He knew that she wasn't going to let up on him, so he was going to have to take that book with him. G-Mama knew that all Rome needed was a push, and when he got his mind set on something, it was no stopping him. So, she would be the person to get it back on his mind. Rome took the book; he was going to question her. He would love to show it to Heaven, so he couldn't be mad. Rome kept checking his phone, and he was about to meet up with Kat. She had something to show him, and it was life or death. He knew that going to see her was a bad mistake, but he felt sorry for her. She said that she had something that would get him sent to jail, and if she didn't show up, Kat would have delivered it to the police herself. She had his attention, and he had to show up, and hoped that it wasn't another one of her mind games.

G-Mama walked into the kitchen and came back out with a plate of food. Rome chuckled. He didn't have time to eat, and he saw the face of G-Mama and picked up his fork. He sent Kat a text saying that he would be late. He knew better to tell G-Mama that he didn't have time to eat her food; he wasn't that stupid. He reached into his pocket and pulled out a wad of cash. She picked it up and tossed it back to him.

" What's that? Where you get that damn money from? You know damn well, I don't want that blood money, and neither should you. Rome, I know you ain't out there slanging that shit?" G-Mama asked.

" Naw, I would never do that, I've been saving. That's all legal money, so take the money old lady," Rome said playfully. He picked the money up and placed it in her hand.

" You were saving? Don't play with me, Rome. I….." G-Mama was cut off by Rome.

" G-Mama, take the money. Let me look out for you for once that ain't no blood money. That's from Heaven and me; it's all legit," Rome lied. She needed help with the bills, and he couldn't sit back and do nothing. If she didn't take it, he would go and pay the bills himself.

She took the money and placed it in her bra, G-Mama knew that he was lying. She wasn't going to push the issue, and G-Mama would take the money and give it to the help center. They could do some good with the money, and she would be proud to give it to them.

" I have to go, G-mama. My shift is about to start; I'm going to make you proud one day, watch you'll see," Rome said, taking one last bite of the food.

" Rome, you not going to finish your food. Be careful out there," G-Mama said worriedly.

Rome got up and kissed the side of her face and chuckled. He could see that she was worried and reassured her that everything was fine. He grabbed his book and walked out of the house. He was on his way to see Kat, and hoped that it wasn't a game, or he would kill her his damn self. He drove off with the music blasting and bobbing his head. He wanted to make his G-Mama proud, and he stared at the book, it had him thinking now.

#

Kat had an ace up her sleeve, and she played every angle that she had, but none of it worked. She was smarter than people gave her credit for, Kat was holding on to a recording that was placing Rome at the scene the day Gotti's goons was murder. She could have easily given that tape to Bugs, and Gotti to save her life, but instead, Kat was taking a gamble, and wanted to gain every dollar she could with what she had. It wouldn't make sense to go through all that bullshit, and she could have just given the tape up.

The power of the dollar always made people do stupid things, Kat knew Rome was responsible for all the money that was taken from Reese, and he wanted her cut. She had family down in Miami, and Kat thought it was time for a change in scenery. Any average person would have given Bugs that tape without even thinking, but Kat played the long game, and weighed every option. She sat in her parked car and waited for Rome to show up.

It was other reasons than money why she held the tape for so long, Kat still cared for Rome, and even though, he left her for Heaven, she still had some type of love for him. She couldn't see herself ever giving that tape to the cops, but Rome didn't know that, and she was about to use that to her advantage. She grabbed her blunt and lit it; she took a deep pull and inhaled the exotic weed. She blew the smoke on and looked around skeptically. She had to be careful because she was playing with fire, and if she didn't be careful, she would for sure get burnt. Bugs had been calling her since last night, and she didn't pick up for him. He was looking for her, and if she didn't get that money to leave town before he found her, then she would be in deep shit. All Kat wanted was the money, and she would be gone from everyone's life for good. Rome was late, and she shook her head, he was always late, and even now, she wanted him.

She wished that she could feel Rome's dick one last time. But that was a fantasy that would never come true. Kat had smoked more than half of the blunt, and Rome still wasn't there. She pulled out her phone and texted him. Kat was starting to think that maybe he stood her up, and wasn't coming. She looked in her rearview mirror, and she could see his white Mercedes pulling up. She started to check her hair, and made sure her hair was fixed correctly. She didn't know why she was doing all that, but it was something Rome did to women that made them act crazy. It was a gift he had, and it was more like a curse to him. He stepped out of the car with his hand near his gun, he looked around, and wasn't about to be set up by Kat. He searched every car that was parked on the street, he understood how dirty a woman like Kat was, and being a woman scorned wasn't helping. He got in the car and looked at Kat, ready for her to start talking.

Kat leaned over and tried to hug him, but he pushed her away from him. He wasn't there for that bullshit, Rome wanted to know what was so important, and want exactly did she have on him. That was the only reason that he was here. Kat pulled out her phone and played the message for Rome. He looked at the small screen and started to curse. Rome punched the steering wheel, and chuckled. How she had this footage, he would never know. If she had this, then it was going to be trouble, and calmed himself down and stared into her eyes.

" How did you get this, and what do you want, Kat?" Rome asked.

" I thought you would never ask, and how I got the tape doesn't concern you. But if you must know, I was following you to confront you about Heaven, and something told me to start recording. You got into that house and minutes later, I hear gunshots, and guess who comes running out," Kat played the tape and tried to show it to him again.

" I saw it the first damn time, what stopping me from killing you right now, and taking the tape?" Rome asked, seriously.

" I have copies, and you don't want to go to jail. It's an innocent man in jail for some shit you did, I don't give a shit about Reese, but his money that's another story. I want a hundred thousand, and I'm gone. You'll never see me again," Kat explained.

Rome looked at her with hate in his eyes, and Kat was a prime example of how the hood would do you. He had the hundred thousand, but he didn't want to give it to her. He was about to hit Gotti, and he would have more than enough to provide her with the money. " Look, I'll give you the cash, but you have to give me some time. Once, I give you that money; I don't want to ever see you again."

" We can have had something special, and you gave that up to be with her," Kat said.

" I already have something special; I want all the copies, Kat. I'll call you when I have the money," Rome got out the car.

She watched him walked away, and she could feel butterflies in the pits of her stomach. Kat started to sweat, and Rome still gave her chills. " That nigga know he fine, he still makes this pussy wet. I'm going to miss him."

#

Heaven, Rome, Fatboy, and Jazzy stood outside the courtroom. The day was finally here, and Jazzy was about to take her time, and Heaven was about to accept community service. Jazzy didn't want to seem like she was scared, but she was on the inside. She didn't want to leave her friends, but she had to put on her big girl panties and hold shit down like the bad bitch that she was, that's what she kept telling herself. She would be damn if she let the world see her fold, she held on to Fatboy's hand, and she gripped it tightly. It took years to realize that he was more than a friend; she wasted all this time. She stared into his eyes, and kissed his lips gently. It was no words exchanged, but she didn't need to say anything; they both knew would each other was thinking. Fatboy prayed that she didn't catch a jailhouse case; he knew that Jazzy was in for a long battle. Her temper would be tested, and he hoped that she didn't fuck somebody up bad, and get more time. He needed her to come home.

Rome didn't tell anyone about the video that Kat had, he would take care of it on his on, but G-Mama and his dream book had been on his mind since she gave it to him. He didn't show Heaven yet, but he was starting to think that maybe he could still be the next

Dapper Dan. He could finally become the man his father always said he would be; he owed to him to at least try. He was searching for his purpose in life, and this was it. He could travel the world, showcasing his clothing line. It may have seemed like a farfetched dream, but it could be a reality with all the money he had now, and when he hit Gotti, he would have more than enough to start his company. He would take care of Kat, and he would never see her again. He wanted a break from all the hood shit; it was taking a toll on his life. It would all work out in the end, and he knew that it would. He stared at Heaven's ass through her dress, and he was turned on. That's what he loved about her, after all these years of being around her, he always found her attractive even when she wasn't trying to be cute.

" Damn, you looking good in the dress, let sneak to the bathroom so I can give you some head before court," Rome said, jokingly as he whispered in her ear. She playfully hit him across his arm. Jazzy saw their happiness, and she became sad. She wasn't supposed to even turn herself in early, she was going to miss Fatboy's summer bash, and her going away party. The lawyer tried his best to get her to leave after that, but the judge and the state's attorney was adamant about her going in now. It was nothing anyone could do, her big mouth had caught up with her, and now six months would be gone from her life. Jazzy held her head up high, and wasn't going to cry over spilled milk. She was going to be a boss wherever she went, and no jail walls would ever change that. Jazzy was going to enjoy the last moments she had with her friends, and wasn't going to waste it with tears in her eyes.

Rome was excited about his future, and he was grateful to have G-Mama reminded him of who he was, and the potential he had. He pulled Heaven to the side and held her hands. He kissed her and couldn't imagine a life without her. Heaven could see a sparkle in his eyes, and she hadn't seen that in a while. It was hope, and she was happy to see it back in him.

" What's up. You have that look on your face," Heaven smiled.

" Remember that dream book we made when we were kids, I still have it, and G-Mama gave it to me. We were so optimistic back then and so filled with hope. I was going to be a clothing designer, and you would run the company with me. What if we could still do that? Rome said with excitement.

" Oh, shit! She still had that, and I remember that, we were going to have matching Range Rovers. Mine would be white, and yours would be black," Heaven said, drifting down memory lane.

" You remembered, huh. Matching Range Rovers, I would love to make that happen," Rome said.

" What's stopping us from doing that, Rome. We can still do that, and I know we can. Let's do it, Rome," Heaven said sincerely.

Rome loved that she always had a positive vibe about everything, and he loved that about her. Maybe, she was right. They could have matching trucks one day, and run their own company. " The sky is the limit."

" It's time. Y'all ready?" The small lawyer said, peeking his head out the courtroom. They all looked at each other, and nobody said anything. It was now a reality, and Jazzy had to leave. Fatboy wanted to take her and run, but it wasn't that serious. He always promised to protect her from the world, and he felt so helpless that he couldn't help her.

" I love y'all! Stop that sad shit! I'm going to knock this time out, and a bad bitch will be back on the streets, causing hell. I wouldn't trade y'all for anything, and you guys are the true meaning of friends. Promise me, we will be friends forever," Jazzy spoke from the heart and meant every word.

They all hugged each other in a group, and held it for a while. They were family now, and nothing could break that bond they shared.

" Friends forever!" They all said in unison.

CHAPTER SEVENTEEN

Jazzy didn't have her high priced wigs, or eyelashes on as she got fingerprinted for processing. She wore an orange suit with her hair braided to the back. She got cold stares from the other inmates, but they had no idea that Jazzy wasn't the chick to fuck with right now. Her mind wasn't in the right place, and when she hit the cell block, Jazzy could feel that time slow down. Each minute felt like five. It was something that she would have to get used to being locked up. If she didn't find a routine, the time would consume her quickly. Jazzy had to keep her mind sharp, or she would lose herself in the system. She grabbed her blanket, sheets, plastic toothbrush, and a pillow from the guard. She looked around as everything seemed new to her, Jazzy had been locked up plenty of times, but would always make bail before she would ever get to this point. She thought that it was funny that she was the one who went to jail, and everyone else was free. But she wouldn't take anything back if she could, it was only six months.

The process was longer then she expected. Hours went by, and she was still going for one place to another. She went to see medical, dental, and a bunch of other shit that made no sense to her. Jazzy was ready to lay down to get some rest. It was a lot waiting around in different holding cells for hours before they would move her to the next location. She started early in the morning, and it was now going on midnight. Jazzy was more shocked at how many young girls were being processed with her. It blew her mind, and it was more than usual. They had everything from murders, fraud, drugs, and a plethora of other shit. It was so many girls throwing their life away for no good niggaz you that wasn't going to do shit for them while they were in here. They would move on to the next chick, and that's the part that fucked Jazzy up. She wished it was something to do to save the young girls, and it made her not bitch about her little time she had. The had young girls who had sixty-year sentences.

She finally made it to her cell block, and the lights were off as most of the inmates were sleep or reading inside their small cell. She walked behind the guard as he led her to her cell, he opened the steel door, and Jazzy looked, and she let out a sigh. It was so small, and it was barely any room to walk, it was so cluttered. Her cellmate watched Tv with her headphones on, and she looked up at Jazzy taking her earplugs out. The guard pushed her inside, and Jazzy placed her stuff on the top bunk. She looked at the sink that was hooked up to the toilet, and she frowned her face up. She would have to drink water from the same pipe that was connected to the fuckin' toilet. She didn't know how she was going to do this, but the upside to it all was how clean the cell was to her. Jazzy could tell whoever her cellmate was that she cared about the cleanliness of her hunt. The girl stood up and leaned against the wall, and nodded her head. Jazzy didn't know what to say, and this girl was a complete stranger to her.

She nodded her head back, and turned her back on the girl. She placed her stuff in her bed, and started to put on her sheets. She didn't say anything yet because she didn't want to fight her first day inside. Jazzy figured that she would mind her business. All she had to do was stay out the way, and she would be fine. But it was more to it than that; she was about to learn that.

" My name is Nya; what they book you on?" She asked, sitting down.

" I'm Jazzy, and I have an assault case on this ugly ass, dirty ass, bitch! I only have six months, something light," Jazzy explained.

" Your first time locked up, huh. You're green. I can see it all over your face. Don't tell anyone that you have only six months, and these hatin bitches will try and get you more time. It's girls in here doing twenty years; they don't want to hear that shit. You bangin?" Nya reached into her box and pulled out a bunch of hygiene products. " Here take this, that bullshit they gave you is no good."

" Bangin'? Naw, that ain't my style. You have to be no more than twenty years old, what are you doing in here?" Jazzy asked.

" I was framed, I'm in here for a dirty ass nigga! You might know him, or whatever. His name is Gotti. He had me take a gun charge for him and left me for dead. Doesn't answer my calls, no visits, no money, he's a real bitch boy!" Nya said, getting angry talking about it.

" Gotti! Yeah, I know that nigga! I hate him!" Jazzy hopped on her bunk and laid down. She was so tired that she could barely keep her eyes open. She missed her friends already, but she missed Fatboy even more. She prayed that this time would fly by.

" I know you are tired. I'll teach you the ropes tomorrow. Get some rest," Nya sat down on the bed and turned the light off.

Jazzy leaned over the bunk. " How much you know about, Gotti? I have some friends on the outside that can make give you a lot of money for info."

Nya had been praying for the day to pay Gotti back for what he did to her. " Everything! I'd give that up for free."

#

" I miss her already, Rome. This shit is my fault," Heaven said, sitting on the passenger side seat. She was living the dream, and her friend was locked up behind some shit with Kat. She had supervision, and community service. It didn't seem right that she was out free while Jazzy was in some bullshit cell. She knew that her bitch would hold things down, but that was beside the point. Heaven felt that she should have been locked up right with her; that's how it was supposed to go when you were best friends. She had been reading the dream book that Rome and her made when they were kids all day. She was on board of them starting their clothing company; Heaven spent most of her life working for someone else. It was only twenty-four hours in a day, and she slept six hours of that, so that was a lot of time wasted building another's person dream. She wasn't going to do that anymore; Jazzy didn't want her job back. Jazzy was taking a page out the late great Nipsey Hustle, and wanted to control her destiny with ownership of her shit. Her brain was moving so fast that she couldn't even think straight.

Rome wasn't listening to a single word she said, it wasn't on purpose, but his mind was focused on Peanut. He was one of Gotti's soldiers, and it was his way to the money. If he was going to rob Gotti, he was going to need someone on the inside, and that was Peanut. Everyone knew that he wasn't built for the street life, and if he ever got locked up, he would be the first to start snitching. Rome was about to offer him a deal of a lifetime, and he knew that Peanut wouldn't pass it up. The dollar bill could convince your own friend to kill you these days. It was a cold world, and that was the main reason Rome didn't move with a bunch of niggaz. He only had one friend coming up, and that was Heaven. They used to make fun of Rome because of that, and he didn't give two shits. He would fight anyone who had something to say about it, that's who Rome was, he always moved off his own pace. He was waiting for the perfect time to approached Peanut, but he had to give it to the little nigga. He didn't move and sold the product until it was gone.

" I got your ass now," Rome said, placing his sunglasses on, and Heaven did the same. He started the car up and followed Peanut as he walked up the street. He made sure to stay back as far as he could to avoid being seen. Heaven and Rome both had on black hoodies. He tried to get her to stay back, but it was like talking to a wall. She didn't listen to him, and Heaven was staying by his side. She was down for the consequences, whatever they may have been. Rome was her future husband, and she was already taking her vows literally. That's how she moved, and Rome loved that shit about her. Rome pulled over as he saw Peanut stop and go into an alleyway; he figured that this was his time to get him. He grabbed his gun from underneath his seat and tucked it at his waist. Heaven was about to open her door and get out with him, but Rome frowned up his face and pushed her back. He let her come, but he definitely wasn't about to let her go with him. Anything could happen, and protecting Heaven meant more to him, then any money could.

" Aht! Aht! Fuck you think you are going? Hold shit down from right here," Rome demanded. She smacked her lips and waved her hand. Rome walked across the streets into the alley with his hoodie over his head. He held his head down low, and put the gun to the back of Peanut's head as he pissed next to a light pole. Peanut felt the cold steel against his head, and he froze up. He thought that his life was over.

" Don't move, motherfucka! You know what this is, nigga! This shit can go one of two ways, I can put a bullet in your fuckin' head, or you can help me rob Gotti, and I'll give you a cut. What's it going to be, nigga?" Rome held on to the gun tightly.

" Wha..what?" Peanut stuttered. " Rome? Nigga, I know your voice! I don't have shit to do with want you and Gotti got going on; let me go, man!"

" You heard what the fuck he said, nigga!" Heaven said, holding a small-caliber gun.

" Didn't I tell your ass to stay in the car, I almost shot your ass creeping' up on me like that, and where the hell you get a gun from? I didn't give you that," Rome looked around cautiously. It was the middle of the day, and they were holding a nigga at gunpoint.

" Jazzy gave it to me!"

" Yo, y'all want me to give y'all a second!" Peanut said.

Rome smacked him in the head, and Peanut fell to the floor. " Look, either you help me or die! You know what, how about I tell the hood that you and

Gotti be ridin' that horse on the old town road. I know he's had you," Rome said, bluffing.

" How you know that? What I gotta do, Rome, and how much I get?" Peanut asked.

" I want to know what day he does inventory and where the cash is going to be at? Feel me? It'll be the easiest money you ever made, and I'll keep your secret that you are a butt pirate, everyone wins," Rome chuckled.

" Okay, man! Just keep your damn mouth close. I got you, how will I find you?" Peanut asked.

" You don't, I'll find you!"

#

" That bad wig-wearing, hoe! I'm going to fuck that bitch up again," Heaven screamed. She was tired of hearing Kat's name, and didn't understand why she wouldn't go away. She was trying to blackmail her man for some money, and that wasn't sitting well with her. Rome sat calmly as Heaven talked her shit, and his mind he was thinking about wedding dates, she was the only one that he cared about. He knew he would have to wait until Jazzy came home from jail, but Rome didn't want to wait; he didn't want to spend another second on earth without her being his wife. He was starting to think that maybe robbing Gotti wasn't the best thing to do, and he was seeing things differently now. He had a future to worry about now with Heaven. Rome had a meeting with someone they could help him with his clothing line

"West Avenue." He was nervous because he still didn't think that he could actually do that; he shook his head at Heaven. She was still going off about Kat, and he needed her to relax. Rome had no problem paying her to leave him the hell alone and give him the tapes she had on him. Rome held onto Heaven's hand as they walked down the block. Rome knew that he was going to miss his hood, but in order for him to make it, he had to leave.

He smacked her on the ass and wanted to take her inside and taste her sweet pussy. His face changed as he saw yellow tape, and the entire neighborhood was surrounded at the corner of the block. Heaven and Rome had just walked out of their house and had no idea what was going on. They were so caught up on their own shit; they never saw or heard anything out of the usual. But clearly, something happened, and Heaven stopped talking about Kat. They both walked down to the end of the corner with the rest of the people. He could see G-Mama standing with her gown on and her silk scarf wrapped around her head. Police and news cameras were everywhere. He looked at Heaven, and his heart dropped from his chest. Rome looked at the teenage boy lying in a puddle of blood with gunshot holes all in his body. He knew the boy, and his name was Mel. Everyone knew him; he was a smart kid with a promising future. He was killed by a Police Officer claiming that Mel reached for something after being mistaken for a game member. Mel wasn't affiliated with anyone, and Rome tried to find out what happened. But everyone was yelling and screaming; the block was in chaos.

They didn't have the decency to covered Mel's body up, and it turns out that Mel was unarmed, and didn't even have a cell phone on him. Heaven shook her head and started to cry. She couldn't raise a child in this madness. Heaven couldn't imagine if that was her child lying on the ground that was killed for no reason. She was even more afraid to tell Rome that she was pregnant, Heaven didn't want to add extra pressure on him. Rome would do anything for her, even if it meant putting himself in danger. If she tells him now, and it would only put him down a darker path, she didn't want to steer him away from his dreams, which was also hers. Heaven didn't tell anyone, but Jazzy. She was the only one who knew; Heaven told her before she went away to prison. Heaven was scared out of her mind; it was so many killings that how could she let her child grow up here. She understood that the hood had so many good things going on, but the killings had to stop. It was ruining the community, and being a black man didn't help.

G-Mama shouted and demanded that they covered the young boy up. She was face to face with the Police Officer, and she punted her finger in his face. Rome pulled her back, and didn't want her to get arrested. She wasn't having it, and she snatched away from Rome and continued to yell. The entire block was getting rowdy, and things were about to turn bad quickly. Rome was starting to lose his cool too, he was trying to calm everyone down, but that wasn't working. Mel was a good kid, and for his life to be ended like that wasn't right.

" G-Mama, calm down! The already killed Mel, please don't make them start shouting again," Rome asked.

" I was a little girl when I saw Dr. King march. These pigs don't scare me, and they kill him for nothing! Absolutely nothing, Rome," G-Mama started to cry, and her words stuttered.

" I know, I know," Rome didn't know what else to say. The pain the hood was feeling right now; he understood it. This wasn't right by a long shot.

" How are we supposed to raise our baby in this shit, if it ain't the police trying to kill us, it's niggaz like Gotti trying to kill us," Heaven spoke from her heart as a tears fell from her eyes. She blurted it out and didn't even know that she said it.

" Wait. What? Our baby? Are you pregnant, Heaven?" Rome asked.

" Yes, I was going to tell you when all this stuff was over," Heaven smiled.

" I'm going to be a daddy! Wow!" Rome was excited, but it was hard to enjoy with Mel lying dead in the streets. He held on to Heaven and G-Mama, it was a sad day for the hood, they had lost one of their own, and it was nothing they could do about it. G-Mama led the large group in prayer, and they all held

the head low. It was all they could do is pray for
better times.

CHAPTER EIGHTEEN

" Chow time! Chow time!" The guard yelled out, and Jazzy sat up on the top bunk, lost in her thoughts. Two weeks went by, and she was counting the days down until she was able to leave this hell hole. She wasn't going to get used to this no matter how much Nya showed her the ropes. Jazzy lost weight because of her refusing the eat anything; it would take some time for her to get used to the food. Hunger always win, and eventually, she would stuff the mystery meat down her throat. The food lacked seasoning, and it was only a small portion, not enough to feel a small child. The only good thing that came out of this was all the information that Nya had on Gotti. Jazzy had been here all this time and still hasn't had a phone call, it was on lockdown, but the unit was released today. She couldn't wait to call him and talked to Fatboy. She missed him more and more each day that went by, more importantly, Jazzy had the keys to getting everything from Gotti. His money was buried behind Nya's house. At least it was there before she got locked up for him. Nya was Gotti's main chick, and they even talked about marriage. But it was all a lie; Gotti used her as his beard to had the fact of him being gay. He used her until he couldn't anymore, and when the pressure was on, he let her go down for his gun and bullshit.

She hadn't received one phone call, or visit from him. Nya tried calling, but the number changed. Now that she knew everything about him being on the downlow, she was mad at the signs that were right in front of her face. Gotti never really wanted to fuck her pussy. He would beg her for anal, and it was all he wanted. It all made so much sense to her now, and she got mad thinking about how she was betrayed. Nya gave up every single detail, and even the sports shop that had, it was a front of all the money that he laundered. Nya didn't leave out one single detail about all of his businesses. She did his books, and the money that she didn't report to the IRS was in the millions now. One anonymous call from whoever and his ass was fried. Nya did most of her time, and was scheduled to go home in a few months. She was done with him, and would get her life back that was taken from her.

" You not going to eat?" Nya asked. Jazzy shook her head; she was getting by eating the boiled egg and a slice of bread that she got at breakfast time. She didn't care about anything, but her phone call. She knew that this info she had would be useful, at least that's what she hoped. She wanted to hear her friend's voice, and Jazzy wanted to see the social worker. Nya told her how to knocked time off her sentence and could be home in sixty days. She had to get out of this place; she didn't know how long she could make it. The time wasn't the issue, but the people that she was around. She saw the stares she got, and she didn't want to be fighting. Jazzy wasn't trying to go down that road, but she would be damn of a bitch was going to try and fuck with her. She hopped off the top bunk and waited for the door to opened. She was only going to chow this time because she needed to get out of her cell; she was tired of being cramped up. Jazzy hated this place, and getting a chance to walked somewhere was more important than eating the bullshit food. Jazzy wanted to kill Kat, and it was that bitch fault that she was in this position. It was more than just Kat, and Jazzy knew it. The door buzzed and it unlocked, she stepped out with a mean mug on her face.

" You can have my food, when we get that phone call?" Jazzy asked. She kept her eyes focused on a big bitch, names Beth. She had been staring at Jazzy since the doors open. She didn't show one ounce of fear, and stood her ground. They were gladly mistaken for thinking that Jazzy was going to fold.

" You sure? Aye, you can trade the food for other shit," Nya explained.

"" I'm good; money is not a problem for me. If you need anything, let me know, I'll have my people fill your books up," Jazzy said, never taking her eyes off big Beth. She approached Jazzy, and she was ready to pop off.

" You Jazzy, right? Big Beth said.

" Yeah, why? If you think that I won't fuck you up, then you got another thing coming!" Jazzy shouted.

" It's not like that, I have something from Fatboy," Big Beth pulled out a small flip phone and discretely gave it to her and walked off. Jazzy looked at the phone and smiled. She walked back in her cell, and decided to skip dinner; she wasn't going to eat anyway.

" Your man got it like that?" Nya asked.

" I guess so, I'm going to skip chow," Jazzy hopped back on her bunk and placed the phone underneath her pillow. She couldn't believe that Fatboy got a phone on the inside. Jazzy knew that she had to be careful, or she would get more time for having a phone. She didn't care at the moment, and had a chance to call her people. How could she not accept that? Jazzy smiled devilishly and dialed Fatboy's number.

#

" *Are you sure, Jazzy? Damn, ain't that some shit, I'm going to check that shit out, I miss your crazy ass, bitch! I can't wait until you come home,*" Heaven said, talking to Jazzy for the first time since she left. She wished that her friend was still here, but hearing her voice brought her nothing but joy. Heaven talked with smoked filled lungs as she sat on the edge of her bed with her hair in a bonnet. She kept smoking and coughing as she spoke, the phone operator let her know that she had only thirty seconds left. Heaven hated that her friend had to go to jail for her shit with Kat, and now she wanted to extort money out of them. Heaven never wanted to kill a person before, Jazzy hung the phone up and walked back to her cell; she didn't want to use her secret phone until the night time. It was fewer guards walking around. Heaven stood up from the bed and sat her blunt down after taking one last pull. She wanted to call Rome and tell him the info she had on Gotti, or she could handle it herself. Heaven was way out of her league, and she knew it. But she figured what if she could pull this off on her own. It would prove her worth to Rome, and that was her ill way thinking from being with Reese.

She didn't have to do that with Rome, and far as he was concern, he was the one that needed to prove his worth to her. Heaven quickly got that shit out her head, and leaned over kissing the side of Rome's face as he slept. She playfully pushed him, waking him up out of his sleep. He looked at her like she was insane; he spent hours on hours working at the hot dog stand. Rome finally caught a break and was getting off parole early. He had one week left, and he started to smoke heavy, now that he was about to be a free man. Rome smelled the high-grade weed and searched around for it. He took it from the table and took a deep pull. Heaven looked at his muscular frame alone with his six-pack, and she wanted to ride his dick. She grabbed it through his basketball shorts, and he smiled. Heaven almost lost focus, and it clicked back in her mind. She began to tell him everything thing that jazzy told her, and he had a massive smile on his face. Rome couldn't be happier now that he was about to be a father.

He had too much to fight for now, and it was crazy. How could he not be there for his family, and Rome thought about his mother. He would never treat his child the way his mother did him; Rome wanted to be there for his kids like G-Mama was for him. Seeing Mel laying in the street did something to his soul, he had to get the fuck out the hood. It was the only way; he was determined to be somebody. Rome wasn't going to let the streets beat him, and being another nigga dead, wasn't going to happen. He placed his ear on her belly, hoping to hear something, Heaven giggled and hit Rome across his head. Rome would take care of everything during Fatboy's summer bash, and it would give him the perfect cover to do what he needed to do and get back safely to his family. He would pay Kat for the tapes she had, and that would be the end of that. Rome could move on with his life and raise his child. He didn't care if it was a girl or boy; it didn't matter to him.

He stood up and began to put on his clothes, the party was tonight, and he had to prepare himself for what was about to go down. He wished he could stay and make love to Heaven, but he had a surprise for her. Rome bought two Range Rovers, one black, and the other one was all white. She was going to be so happy, rarely in life, everything you wish for comes true, Rome shrugged his shoulders. He thought that he had to be one lucky motherfucka.

" I got something I want to show you, put some clothes on. After tonight, our life will change for the better, and I promise never to let you down. If something doesn't go right, I want you to take the money and leave this city. My child deserves better," Rome explained.

Heaven got up from the bed. " You're scaring me, Rome, nothing is going to happen. Jazzy gave us the nail in the coffin, we got him, baby."

" Promise me, Heaven," he said seriously.

" Okay, bae. What do you have to show me," Heaven quickly places on her clothes and couldn't wait? She loved that he was spontaneous, and she jumped on his back.

" It's a surprise; it's outside, go down and see," Rome smiled.

Heaven and Rome walked outside, and she started to run when she saw the two Range Rovers sitting in front of the house. One was all white, and the other was black. Heaven's had a red bow wrapped around the truck, she looked at him and figured how did she get a man like, Rome. She planted soft kisses all over his face, and snatched the keys out his hand as he dangled them in front of her face.

" Damn, I wish Jazzy was here for this! How'd you do this without me knowing, Rome? Oh, my god. I love you!" Heaven opened the door, and she sat down inside.

Rome looked at Heaven, and it was no better feeling than seeing her with so much joy. His job was to keep her happy, and without her, he was nothing. She was the reason for his being, and Rome knew it. He had a bad feeling in his heart that something was going to go right. He still was going to go through with it, Rome should have listened to her inner self because shit was about to hit the fan.

#

Bugs and Gotti rode around with weed smoked floating throughout the car. Gotti was tired of waiting, and wanted Rome dead. His jealousy had been taken to another level, he heard all the moves he's was making on the streets, and it only made him angrier. He tried to let things play out, but Gotti was done sitting back, he didn't want to kill his friend. But in his mind he didn't have a choice, he was the man on the streets, and Rome had played him for a fool. He didn't see the issue with what he did, money was money, and he wasn't not going to work with Reese because of him. He didn't understand why Rome was so upset about that, and it was more to the story to Rome. The line was crossed when Gotti tried to force himself on him. Gotti told himself that to feel better about the situation, but he knew why. He wanted to be with Rome, and he couldn't have him. Gotti wanted Heaven out the picture, but he couldn't tell Bugs the real reason. So, Gotti kept the lie going, and he would never live his truth. He would keep the secret with him until the day he died. Gotti was ready for the world to knew who he really was, and but they never would.

They had been everywhere looking for Kat, and Bugs had promised that she would deliver Rome. It wasn't turning out that way; Kat wasn't answering the phone for him. She had the key to giving them Rome, but she was holding it to her chest. Kat risked her life for the money, and like most people, the cash would make you do crazy things. She had an opportunity not to be broke anymore, and Kat couldn't pass that up. The clock was ticking, and she was playing chicken with a moving car, and that moving car was Bugs. He didn't care about anything, and didn't value life at all. Bugs had no problem taking a life, and it came all so natural to him. Kids, women, old ladies, it didn't matter to him. Murder was murder, and nobody was exempted in his book. He had no code, and that's why Gotti kept him around, he would do the dirty work that everyone else was scared to do. Bugs puffed his blunt and pulled his car up to Kat's house. He didn't see her car parked in front because it was in the back. He could see the light on through the window.

He grabbed his gun from his waist, Gotti stayed in the car as he watched Bugs get out. He didn't want to see what was about to take place. Gotti wasn't a killer, but he kept them around him. He didn't have the heart to kill a woman, or anyone else for that matter. He had killed before, but it wasn't in him, and only would do it if it was necessary. Bugs crept up to the house and peeked in the side mirror. He rang the doorbell and didn't get an answer. Bugs was itching to kill something, he knew that Kat would never deliver, and he would get a chance to use his gun. Bugs had been begging Gotti to kill Rome since he got out of prison. He didn't like all the love that Rome got from the streets. They treated him like he was a god, and Bugs didn't like that shit at all. Bugs was done waiting, so he walked around to the back door and placed his hand on the door handle, and it was open. He shook his head that it was unlocked. Kat had taken the garbage out and forgot to lock the door back.

" Stupid, bitch," Bugs mumbled. He walked inside the house, and he could hear Kat singing. She had on her Apple Air Pods and was taking a bath. She was soaking her body, and didn't know that Bugs was inside the house. He walked right past the laptop that sat on the table with everything they needed to bring Rome down. That laptop contains all that he needed to put Rome away for life, and Bug walked right past it. He made his way to the bathroom and stood at the doorway.

Bugs watched her like a creep for a few seconds admiring Kat's naked body. Kat's eyes were closed, and Bugs cleared his throat. Kat felt like she saw a ghost, and she stared at the gun that was in his hands.

" Bugs, what the hell are you doing in my house?" Kat shouted.

" Times up, bitch! You got something on Rome or not! I'm not playing with you right now," Bugs cocked the hammer back on his gun.

" I told you I need some more time; all I need is a little more. I'm close, Bugs," Kat lied. She thought about the laptop and the video she had, but her greed had her mind cloudy. She felt that she could talk her way out of it again, and get the money from Rome.

" I don't have time! Do you have anything! Last time I'm going to ask you!"

Kat tried to stand up and make a sexual advance, but even that wasn't going to work. " Let me suck your dick and get the stress off you."

Bugs smiled and fired a shot, and her dead body fell back into the tub. Her brains flew onto the back wall. The water turned red as she slumped low in the tub. Bugs tucked his gun back at his waist and walked back past the laptop that could have gotten Rome.

#

Rome had a duffel bag filled with the money that Kat asked him for, and it was his last. The money he got from Reese, the last of it, he was about to give to Kat to get that video back. Everything depended on him hitting Gotti now, Rome was betting on himself. He was driving with his designer shades blocking the bright sun, and his partner in crime, Heaven sat next to him. She wasn't going to let him go see Kat by himself. She didn't care how pregnant she was that shit wasn't going to happen on her watch. If it were left up to her, they wouldn't give Kat shit. Heaven hated Kat with a passion; she didn't have a soul, and didn't care who life she hurt. The money was the only thing she cared about, Heaven always said that Kat wasn't in love with Rome, but the potential that he possessed. It was clear the Rome future was bright, and the moment he realized it, the possibilities would be endless. Heaven was reluctant about leaving the hood, and they were raised here. But now she knew that Rome was right; it was time for them to spread their wings and fly.

The world was waiting for them, and the only thing holding them back was the hood. Rome was hoping that Kat was at home; it wasn't like her not to pick up for him. He left her several voicemails about him having the money, Rome decided to give it to her now. He already talked to his P.0. about being transferred to California, and once he hit Gotti, he was going to be in the wind. Rome was closing all the chapters in his life that was still open. He talked with G-Mama, and she was happy for Rome. She was happy that Rome was leaving, and the only person Rome had to see was his mother. He had to let her go, Rome couldn't live his life being guilty about her getting high. He had to live his life for himself now, that was a hard conversation he was going to have, but he was ready to have it. Rome didn't want this life anymore, he stared at the gun on his lap, and then at Heaven's belly. She wasn't showing yet, but he knew which one he had to pick. Rome would kill anyone who stood in his way from being there for his child.

He gripped the steering wheel tightly and pulled up to Kat's house. He knew that she had to be inside, and had been over enough to know that her back door was always opened. He never understood why she never locked it, that was mind-blowing to him. Rome tucked his gun and looked over at Heaven, and by the look, she was giving him, it was no way she was staying in the car. He wasn't going to even waste his time trying to convince her. Heaven smacked her lips and looked at him like he was crazy. Rome couldn't help but laugh, and kiss her on the lips. He hoped that this was the end between Kat and him, Rome knew that he made mistakes with her, and wanted to leave that all behind him now. If she could take the money and leave him the fuck alone, he would be the happiest man on the planted. Rome looked around; he was always cautious about his surroundings. He took a deep breath and mumbled to himself.

" Let's get this shit over with, and control yourself, Stinky," Rome looked at her, and Heaven rolled her eyes. They stepped out of the car, and the bag filled with money was on his shoulder. He went straight to the back door and didn't even ring the doorbell. He saw her that the door was cracked and slowly opened the door. Heaven wanted to smack him on the back of his head, and he knew exactly how to get in, and that slightly pissed her off.

" Your ass would know how to get in this hoe house, ain't that some shit," Heaven said.

" Oh, so you going to go there, wow," Rome laughed. He was creeping through the house, trying not to be heard.

" Where the fuck you at, bitch? Bring your ass out! Hello!" Heaven was yelling, walking throughout her house. She didn't know why Rome was creeping, Heaven wasn't playing, and Rome wanted to do this and leave. " Fuck, are you a cat burglar? Let's get this over with already!"

" Kat! Kat!" Rome called out. They both made their way up the stairs; Rome spotted the laptop, and grabbed it. He held onto it, and they started to search upstairs. He thought that maybe she wasn't here, but he was shocked once he walked into the bathroom, and the smell was strong.

Kat was slumped over with her head blown off; her phone sat on the floor. She was still in the tub, soaking in bloody water, and Rome covered his mouth and tried to block the smell. Heaven had a smile on her face and didn't flinch at the dead body.

" That bitch dead, and her wig still is on crooked, man that shit always irritated me, Rome. Why you ain't never tell her about that bogus ass wig," Heaven said.

" Stinky, really? She's dead! I think that you should let that go now!" Rome chuckled.

" God, don't like ugly! Look at you, bitch!" Heaven said, talking to Kat like she could hear her.

Rome didn't know what the fuck happened in here, but searched every inch of her house and took all her phones and the laptop. He wiped the place down clean of everything he may have touched. He walked out of the house with his bag of money on his shoulder and drove off without a care in the world.

CHAPTER NINETEEN

Fatboy's Summer Bash......

The block was cluttered with people from every hood, and they showed up for the biggest party of the summer. It was the annual summer bash that he would throw to close the summer off, the music blasted loudly, and it looked like a scene out of the movies. Food, liquor, and even some big-time rappers showed up to perform, and it was free to attend. Fatboy paid for everything out his pocket, and that's why the hood loved him so much. Usually, Fatboy would be wherever the bad chicks were at, but not this time. He could barely enjoy himself, and he missed Jazzy with every fiber of his being. None of this meant anything to him anymore, and he saw life differently. Jazzy had changed him, her not being here to party with him was not sitting well with him. Fatboy felt guilty and figured that he shouldn't be having fun without his other half. He had been turning women down the entire night, and ruining the dreams of all the gold diggers that thought they were about to snatch him up tonight. He sipped his

Hennessy from his red plastic cup, and gave dap to people as he moved through the crowd. Fatboy welcome everyone, but Gotti's people, he didn't need any trouble tonight.

It was all about having fun, and all that petty hood beef could be put on hold for the night. He smiled as he saw Rome and Heaven. They walked looking like celebrities dripped in Balenciaga from head to toe, but their mind was only on one thing, and that was the robbery that was about to take place. Rome and Heaven wanted to be seen in case some shit went down. Rome left out a crucial part of his plan to Heaven, and he wasn't going to take her. But Heaven knew Rome like the back of her hand, and she knew that he would try and leave her. She wasn't having that shit, and would be right there with her man. She could smell the palm trees and California already. Heaven was ready to get the hell out of there, and start their company up. They both knew that it was going to be a lot of work, but anything was better than not doing anything. They weren't going to sit back and let time fly past in hood doing the same shit every day, that wasn't life. Heaven saw the look on Fatboy's face, and they both shared the same pain. It wasn't the same without Jazzy, she hugged him, and they both smiled. Rome spotted Peanut talking to some girl, and he checked his watch. Peanut was early, and Rome hoped that he had the information that he needed, or shit would get ugly fast.

Peanut kept looking over his shoulder because he knew that at any moment, Fatboy could see him. Everyone knew that he was rolling with Gotti, but the liquor and the drugs were flowing, and nobody gave a fuck. Rome walked over a snatched him up by his collar; he was smooth and swift with it. He didn't want to draw any unwanted attention to peanut, or he would be a dead man. Heaven slowly moved away from Fatboy, and she didn't want him to see Peanut. She wanted to keep an eye on Rome too; he thought he was slick and was going to try and leave him. That shit wasn't happening; she loved that he looked out for her. Heaven would forever be his Stinky; he gave her happiness that no other man had done before. It was a beautiful thing the witness with them. The friendship that they had made it work; it prepared then for the relationship they were in now. She could barely hear herself think because of the loud music. She nodded her head as one of her favorite rappers hit the stage. She could see Jazzy dancing in her mind now, and she laughed.

" The fuck you doing here so early, nigga! I gave you a certain time and place to be, nigga. You trying to set me up?" Rome shoved his gun in Peanut's mouth. Heaven pussy got wet, and it turned her on when he did his thing. She watched him get on his gangster shit with Peanut. That alone made her want to give him her love box.

Peanut snatched back and looked around. " I had to motherfucka! Aye, I'm helping you out, and stop pointing the gun at me. You kill me, and you won't have shit. The money is on the move, only one guy, and he's in a Dodge caravan. I know the route and time it will be at this red light. Gotti doesn't play about time, and trust me; the van will be there. If you let them get that money to the spot, you'll never get it. They'll kill you instantly, and it's no getting in there. You got one try, or it's over," Peanut explained. He was clueless about the info Rome had from Nya and Jazzy. Rome had everything on Gotti, and when he was through, he wouldn't have shit left to him.

" You sure? I'd you're lying, I swear I'm going to kill you slowly," Rome said.

" You are running out of time, and if I were you, I would leave now. Where's my money, I told you everything I know," Peanut held his hand out.

" I'll pay you when the job is done, text me all the information now. If what you say is true, then you will get paid. I'm a man of my word."

Peanut texted Rome's phone with the time and address, and Rome didn't have much time. He looked at Heaven and knew it was no ditching her, so he just nodded his head and walked off to his car. He popped the trunk open, and it was all black gear with an automatic shotgun. Rome took the ski mask out, and they drove off.

#

Rome waited with his all-black attire on with Heaven sitting in the driver seat. His automatic shotgun sat in his lap, and his heart was beating fast, Rome was nervous, but ready to get this shit over with now. He checked the time that was on the radio, and was starting to think that maybe Peanut lied to him and was setting him up. He had to get this money; everything was falling in place, and this was the last piece to the puzzle. He had a flight booked to California already, and he would visit his mother one last time, then he was gone in the wind. That was the plan, but shit never went as planned, he hoped that it did. He kept his eyes on the mirror, looking for the Dodge van to pull up. He could see that Heaven was nervous too, her legs were shaking, and he placed his hand on it to calm her down. Rome sucked his teeth with anticipation of what was coming next. This was his moment, and nothing was going to stop him from doing this robbery. He thought about all the things he did in his life, and he had to do this, the child in Heaven's belly was all the reason he needed in the world. He could start his company, and the sky would be the limit after that. He was beginning to lose his patience, and he was seconds from leaving with he saw the van approaching. " Game time!" Rome shouted, pulling his mask down his face, and Heaven did the same.

" I love you, Rome," Heaven said. The car slowly pulled up, and the light turned red, it was like the Gods were working with him. The light turned as the car pulled up, and it was perfect timing. Time slowed down, and Rome started to think about everything at that moment; it was like his life flash before his eyes. He could see the future with his child and Heaven. All of his dreams come true, and he could also see the other outcome with him lying dead in the middle of the street with Heaven crying over his lifeless body. Rome still had an opportunity to pull back. He didn't know what to do, and that was killing him. Rome had to do something and do it fast. The van filled with millions of dollars was in front of him, and he couldn't worry about the thoughts that he was having on his mind. It wasn't time to play the guessing game, it was do, or die. Heaven could see that he was about to back out. She supported anything Rome wanted to do, and they could find another way to get the money. She was about to pull him back as she was having the same feelings; something didn't feel right. But she waited too long to tell him, Rome jumped out the car with his shotgun in hand.

" Get the fuck out the car, nigga! You know what this is, let me see those hands," Rome was yelling. In the driver seat was Peanut, and he knew then that it was a setup. It wasn't a single dollar in the van. Rome cursed and waved his shotgun at Peanut, and Rome pulled him out of the driver seat and threw him down to the floor. He had a smile on his face that said it all. Police cars swarmed the from out of everywhere, he looked over at Heaven and waved his hand for her to leave him. She started to cry and started up the car, Rome knew that it was a setup, he could feel it in his stomach, and he went through with it anyway. He kicked Peanut, and his teeth fell out of his mouth. Blood leaked onto the side of his face. The police cars were getting closer, and Heaven didn't have much time left, if she was going to get away, then she needed to leave now. He picked Peanut up and slammed him back down to the ground as hard as he could. He knew that he was going back to jail; another gun charge was a mandatory five years. Rome shook his head, and blew Heaven and kissed. He shook his head, giving her the signal that it was okay, and she should leave.

" Leave now, Stinky! It's okay! Go! Now!" Rome was screaming. He knew that if he had jumped in the car with her, it would have been a car chase. Heaven tears were coming from her eyes, she reluctantly drove off, and the tired made screeching sounds as she drove. She watched in her mirror as the police cars rushed Rome with their guns out.

" No! No! No! Rome!" Heaven yelled.

Rome held his arms up in the air; they surrounded him, ready to shoot him dead at any second. He chuckled because Gotti outsmarted him, Rome was always the most intelligent guy in the room, but not this time. He got out down, and now he was going to back to jail, and his soon to be wife was pregnant. Rome was lost of words, and he had to take this on the chin.

" Get on your knees!" The police officer yelled.

Rome did what he was told, he got on his knees, and they placed him in handcuffs and tossed him in the car. His only thoughts were, did Heaven make it to safety. His mind was racing; he didn't care what happened to him, and needed Heaven to be okay. She was his Stinky, and she deserved better for him. Rome knew that Peanut was a rat, and he did what rats do. Rome would be back better than ever, and he wasn't going to trip. Nobody could stop his greatness; it was his destiny.

#

Sweat dripped from Heaven's head, and she was trying to get a grasp on what the fuck just happened. She rested her head on the steering wheel, and began to cry. Rome was caught by the police, and set up by peanut. Heaven knew something wasn't going to go right, she could feel it, and now Rome was in jail. She didn't know what to do, so she called Fatboy. Her mind was racing, and wasn't going to let Rome go to jail for nothing. She was pregnant, and she could possibly lose Rome for the next five years for having a gun on parole. She could hear the sirens as the police were still out looking for her; she knew that she had to get out of this car. She sniffed and wiped the tears from her eyes. Heaven got her shit together, and drove off. She was told Fatboy to meet her at the address Jazzy gave her, and it was Nya's house. Rome wasn't sure how well he could trust the info that Nya gave Jazzy in prison, and said he would do things his way. Heaven had no choice to see if the money was there; she wasn't about to give up now. They had come too far to let Gotti win, she put on her big girl panties, and kept pushing. She pulled the car up to Nya's house and pulled up in the back. She saw Fatboy sitting in his truck waiting.

Fatboy stepped out the car, and Heaven ran and buried her head in his chest in tears. He was a little upset that they didn't come to him, he told Rome that he would help rob Gotti. But they were his friends, and that was water underneath the bridge to him. He opened the trunk and handed her a shovel, and if it was money in the yard, they were going to find it. Fatboy understood that Rome just got locked up, but he understood the rules that came with this shit, and the game doesn't stop. Fatboy felt the best thing Heaven could do for Rome was get this money. He would handle Bugs, and Gotti for Rome, and his plan was already in motion. They would be dead before the morning, he smiled thinking about how he would blow Gotti's head off his shoulders. It was a long time coming, and now he would give the hood what they have wanted for years, and that was Gotti dead. Heaven had come a long way in a short period of time, and she never thought she would be a part of something like this. But she was in love, and that shit made you do crazy things. She made a promise to hold her best friend, so that's exactly what she was going to do.

She stared at the shovel, and took a deep breath. They both walked into the backyard and looked around skeptically. The block was dry, and everyone was at Fatboy's party. If they were going to do this then they had to be fast, Fatboy started to dig precisely where Jazzy told them to dig. It seemed like it was going to be easy, but it wasn't, and the time was going by slow. They both were breathing heavily, and Heaven kept digging. She was tired, and her arms were burning. Heaven had to finish Rome's plan, and it was the only for them to have a future and build their company. She thought about the baby that was in her stomach, and knew that she had to be better. She could get her mind of Rome; she could only imagine the hurt he was feeling right now. Fatboy smiled as he heard the sound of the metal on metal from hitting a box, and he got down on his knees and started to move the dirt with his hand. He started laughed; they both couldn't believe that Jazzy was right. The money had to be inside; Heaven truly beloved that it wasn't for nothing. She helped him pull it out the ground, the pulled struggled, and finally was able to lift it out. He smashed the lock off with the tip of the shovel.

Fatboy didn't wait any time and cracked it open. Heaven couldn't help but laugh as she stared at all the money, it was neatly wrapped, and she grabbed one of the bundles. She stared at it for a second, and was caught up in the moment. " We did it, baby!" Heaven said. She was talking to Rome even though he wasn't there; Fatboy began to ran back to the truck and grabbed a bag, and start stuff the money inside of it.

" Damn, Jazzy was right! I swear I love that girl! I......." Fatboy's words were cut short as the blast from Bugs gun sent his body flying back.

Bang........Bang.......

Heaven walked over and stood over Fatboy's body, and she put pressure on his shoulder blade. Gotti walked over and smacked Heaven. He picked the bundle of money up from the ground and held it up.

" Y'all think I was going to let Rome rob me, and then you bring Fatboy's stupid ass into this. I wanted Rome to join me, but nah! All he cared about was you, bitch! Now look at him, you were never going to get away with this," Gotti shouted. He poked his chest out, and felt like the kind of the world.

Heaven was on the ground next to Fatboy, and he was only about in the shoulder and the leg. He kept secretly tapping her leg with his gun; Heaven didn't want to seem so obvious and look down. She knew what it was, and she was scared. She wasn't a killer, and knew that she would have to try because they were going to kill her anyway.

" I bet you feel so stupid now!" Bugs laughed. " I think I'm going to have some fun with this bitch before I kill her! Yeah, I think I will!"

Heaven took the gun without thinking and started to shoot. She didn't aim or even try and hit her target. She kept squeezing until the gun clicked, and it was empty. God was on her side because the first shot killed Gotti instantly, and Bugs was hit in the chest. He was gasping for air, and began to cough up blood.

" Did you get them?" Fatboy asked.

" Yeah, I think so!" Heaven stuttered.

Fatboy struggled to get up, and she helped him from the ground. He wrapped his arm around her, and kicked Gotti's dead body. He could barely stand to his feet; he took the gun from Heaven and placed a new clip in and cocked it back. He shot Bugs in the head, and took him out of his misery.

" Get the money, Heaven, let's get the fuck out of here!" Fatboy shouted. " So, what are you going to do now that all this is over?"

Heaven looked at him and smiled. " I'm going to California and continue to live out Rome's dream until he comes home. I'll raise my child and wait for my man. You and Jazzy should come with me."

Fatboy's shook his head. " Yeah, I think I will. New beginnings, huh! Get me out of here before I bleed to death."

Heaven rushed all the money to the car, and she carried Fatboy next, and they rode off into the darkness.

CHAPTER TWENTY

4 Years later....Rome and Heaven's wedding day....

Heaven's daughter, Gianna, tossed flowers down the aisle with a cute sundress on with her hair in two pigtails. Rome stood firm and center with massive smile on his face, he spent a long four years in prison for being caught without another gun. But that was all behind him now, it was his wedding day, and he was marrying his best friend, and soul mate, Heaven. His precious daughter was getting bigger everyday, and the people he loved the most was with him. The beautiful California weather had his spirits high, Rome thanked God every chance he got for sparing his life. He was truly blessed to have a women like Heaven, she held him down sheik he was in prison, and when he was able to leave out the prison gates, Heaven had everything set up for him. They had a successful clothing line called " West Avenue" and he old it all to his wife. She was able to keep his dream alive. He nodded his head at G-Mama, and the look in her eyes gave him the stamp that she was proud of the man he had become. He wasn't a boy anymore, and the hood was in his rearview. He missed it, but he had to let it go.

His mother Lisa was four years sober, and had been clean since the day Rome found her in that abandon building. She was able to to stay clean and now she was sitting front Row at her son's wedding. Fatboy was his best man, and Jazzy was a bridesmaid. He couldn't have asked for a better life, he didn't question God's work. His thoughts stopped as he saw Heaven walking towards him with her father holding on to Heaven. The veil covered her head, and Rome let a tear drop from his eyes. He never saw a women more beautiful then his Queen, he could help but think about the young girl that told him that he was going to be okay when his father died. True love always found a way, Rome, and Heaven was the definition of that. Rome wipe the tear from his cheek and removed the veil from Heaven's head. They mouth were lost in each other's eyes, and didn't know how that got to this point. The love they had for each other was unconditional. Jazzy was smiling from ear to ear, and she whispered in Heaven's ear.

" Yes, bitch," Jazzy said. Heaven giggled. Jazzy was always they same everywhere she went. When she got out she completely opens up to Fatboy, and she gave him her all. Heaven brought everyone out to the west coast with her, it didn't take much convincing to get Jazzy to come. G-Mama on the other hand, it took a lot to get her to leave her neighborhood after being there so long. The preacher spoke and let them exchange vows, and Rome held on to his daughters hand. He placed the ring on her finger, and they both said the magic words " I do."

" And now with the power invested in my, I now pronounce you man and wife. You may kiss your bride," The preacher said.

Rome kisses Heaven and their tongues tangled together in the happiest moment in his life. He held on to his wife hand and picked his daughter up and spun her around. It was the beginning of a lifetime with his Stinky. He had a famiky, and what made it even more special he got to spend it with his mother. Her being sober was the best feeling in the world, Rome looked up at the sky. " This is for you, Pops!"

The time seem like it was flying by as he was sharing the first dance with Heaven. She leaned her head on his shoulder, and it was like they were the only two people in the room. The were lost in the money, Rome never thought his life would turned out like this.

" I love you, Stinky," Rome whispered in her ear.

Heaven smiled and kissed the side of his face. " I love you, too! Us forever!"

Rome looked around the room at all his family. " Us forever."

THE END……

SUBMISSIONS

Looking for a Publishing home? Hit me up if you are looking for a publisher who cares about the author! #DreamWriters Now accepting submissions for street lit, urban romance, urban fiction, etc.... Inbox me or email me at Jaythawriter@gmail.com

Join my mailing list

https://amazon.us18.list-manage.com/subscribe?u=f86fb1f3914d355fa89230b fb&id=d9aff8ac16